ROBIN MUTT:
THE HAUNTED
CLOWN
(13 Tales of Death)

AMY McLEAN

Cover design by Creative Covers

For the unjumbled Robin Mutt

I can't promise the following pages will make sense.

Amy McLean

Contents

Author's Note

I'm fascinated by death.

I realise that, while I'm not entirely alone in that statement, I'm definitely among the minority who would be willing to make such a declaration. My favourite films all feature death. The novels I love either see the demise of certain characters, or begin with their characters already dead. When I first conceived the idea for *Robin Mutt: The Haunted Clown (13 Tales of Death)*, I couldn't believe I hadn't thought of it sooner. To write so abundantly about death, and often with such a kooky and peculiar approach, promised the perfect outlet for the oddities that battled to be unleashed from my imagination.

A few years passed before I finally began it though. Something kept holding me back. That *something*, however, is actually the very reason why I intended to write this collection to begin with. Generally speaking, people shy away from talking about death. This is not something I entirely understand, but I realise I'm one of only a few to so eagerly glorify the subject of death.

However, we are always being encouraged to live life to the fullest, and one cannot have life without having death also. Shouldn't we embrace both together? Of course, it's an emotional subject. It can be testing, challenging, even heartbreaking to contemplate, particularly if a loved one has been lost or an entire community is struggling with a mass devastation. However, no matter how difficult it may be to talk about death, it should never,

ever be awkward.

After all, death is something each and every one of us experiences at some point in our lives. It should be something we can openly and honestly discuss. I have a very clear idea of what I would like done with my own body after my passing, and, while I'm quite content to share this information with those who would be responsible for ensuring that my wishes are fulfilled, I am aware that, for those people, it could be a delicate matter and they may not wish to discuss such a seemingly negative subject.

My death, however, is just as important to me as my life, if not more so. My death is my final mark on the world. This realisation that there is this apparent discomfort surrounding the very conversation made me want to play my part in normalising the concept of death by writing about it.

Death as depicted through art is vast and varied. While this collection contains one or two entries that are a little more serious, a little more realistic, the majority of tales here are quite nonsensical. I think this element of dissociation renders it a little easier to engage with death by distancing it slightly from reality. However, the outcome is always the same: the heart stops beating, the blood stops flowing, and the lungs stop breathing.

I know this won't be for everybody. So many people are unable to even think about the subject of death, however absurd the stories may be, and I totally get that. I really do. But for me, this collection marks not only my first real purge of some of the more peculiar creations that have been festering in the darkest depths of my mind, but also my initial strive to finally feeling free enough to open up the truths of my own fascinations.

Amy McLean

The Batshit

'Have you seen the state of her?'

'I heard they call her the Batshit.'

'Because she's—'

'Batshit crazy? Yeah!'

True enough, Winny had heard the names people called her. She could also quite accurately surmise the whispers that echoed throughout the school behind her back. And it wasn't just in school either: the neighbours called her it; her cousins didn't refrain from it; she even overheard the postman referring to her that way when he thought she was out of earshot.

What people seemed to forget though was that bats had exceptionally powerful hearing. No sound was too discreet for them.

Of course, if one tried to persuade Winny that she wasn't a bat, and that she was in fact a fifteen-year-old human girl, she would shut her hearing down. The part of her brain that could lock out any external noise kicked in uncontrollably, meaning it was completely fruitless trying to communicate with her.

Winny hadn't always been convinced she was a bat. She had a healthy childhood, slightly timid in her youth but always full of smiles. She had been, to want for a better word, *normal*.

But that all changed after she saw the moth.

Barely a teenager and with emotions flying all over the place, Winny had been on edge for a few months as her mind and body struggled to come to terms with one another's hormonal changes.

1

She had been feeling particularly overwhelmed after a rough day at school and had wandered upstairs to take a nap, only to be distracted by the sound of her cat miaowing at something in the bathroom.

She peered around the door to see what was wrong with Fluffy, only to find the feline staring up and yowling at the little moth that was gently fluttering on the ceiling. It was barely two inches wide, silent and almost still, but for some reason Winny flipped. She fled the bathroom, leaving Fluffy to gaze after her in confusion, and flung herself under the bed covers.

In her state of exhaustion and unsettling adolescent transitions, she had been convinced that that tiny winged creature was not a humble moth making a pitstop in her bathroom, but rather a blood-sucking vampire bat that had come to drain the life out of Winny and her family.

It was quite an irrational response, and Winny would have admitted as much once she'd calmed down, had she not drifted off into a deep sleep soon after. With chattering teeth and tears running down her cheeks, she rocked herself back and forth, and didn't wake until morning. If she had only been able to fight through her emotional exhaustion, perhaps her life, her mind, would be entirely different. Still *normal*.

Unfortunately, that's not how it turned out, as that night Winny dreamt that she was a bat. It was just her mind's way of dealing with her sudden irrational fear by forcing her to confront it. After all, facing one's fears was often a recognised method of processing an incident. But for Winny, it turned out to be anything but a harmless exercise.

Now one wouldn't dare suggest that Winny awoke the next morning and flapped off to school with no knowledge that she existed inside a human casing. She was, at that point, still the same Winny she had always been. However, both the moth and Winny's subsequent dream had triggered something in her, a condition that may well have been underlying for many years: with each passing day, Winny became increasingly convinced that she was a bat.

It all seemed safe enough to begin with. She started dressing in dark netted skirts and laced tops. She died her blonde hair a glossy black. She turned to make-up only to blacken the already-dark circles around her eyes and to apply blood-red lipstick onto her lips. The physical transformation was extreme, but it was her mental alterations that would become of greater concern.

Now, Winny's parents weren't neglectful. As soon as they realised there was a problem – which probably arrived around the time Winny started to drink only red liquids as imitation vials of blood – Winny was whisked away to a therapist. And then another. And a few more after that. Nobody seemed to be able to penetrate Winny's absolute belief that she was a bat.

She was kept away from the television. She was home-schooled for a few months. Attempts were made to change her diet, but Winny refused to eat anything that had not at one point been a fresh, juicy, blood-filled animal. Nothing anybody tried seemed to have any effect on her.

And the further away they appeared to stretch from discovering a cure for Winny's problem, the closer Winny came to finishing her project. Winny knew in her heart that she was a bat trapped in a human shell. She was doing everything she could do fulfil her destiny, but she soon realised that there was something very important missing.

Bats could fly. Winny could not.

But Winny wasn't going to let that get in her way. Instead, she was simply going to have to craft her own wings. During the few weeks that followed, she spent every evening after school abandoning her homework (for why would bats need to do homework?) to instead sketch out designs to make her very own set of bat wings.

She collected material samples, tore up some of her clothing to test the strength of different fabrics. She spent her allowance on extra-strength glue and metal rods and pliers and heavy-duty string.

She drew and cut and moulded and reshaped until her project was complete. She just had to let the glue dry overnight and then, the next day after school, they would at last be ready for her to try them out. It was the final phase for Winny to fully morph into the bat she knew she was born to be.

With the excitement of what was waiting for her at home, Winny could hardly concentrate the next day during her lessons back in the classroom. Mathematics was unimportant to her, and she had no use for learning about the Civil War. She didn't need to know about tectonic plates or suffixes or iambs. She paid more attention to the ticking of the second hand as it crawled around the clock face than she did to anything her teachers said. As soon as the bell sounded at the end of the day, she sprung out of her chair, raced across the court, and broke through the school gates.

'Look at the Batshit run!' she heard somebody shout.

'You off to catch a mouse for dinner, Batshit?' another person laughed at her.

Winny was too caught up in her own thoughts to pay her tormenters any attention. Once those wings were strapped onto her back, nothing anybody could say or do would hurt her anymore. She would show them once and for all that she *was* a bat.

Winny knew it wasn't going to be a task without hurdles though. Her first obstacle was to sneak back out of the house again without her parents noticing. They had practically kept her under lock and key over the last few months, realising that her condition was worsening, but unsure of the thoughts that spooled around their daughter's mind since she rarely spoke anymore.

Instead of risking anybody seeing her as she left through the front door, Winny figured it would be safer to climb out of her bedroom window and pull the wings down after her. She landed on the garage roof with a thud, jumped up to grab onto her wings, and allowed them to tumble down onto the roof beside her. They remained intact, a good sign of their robustness, Winny considered as she lowered herself and the wings down onto the ground below.

Phase one: complete.

The walk to the woods from her house would take her a good ten minutes, and she didn't want anybody to see what she was up to in case they told her parents. She had to pull this off. She *had* to. She folded the wings in half and slid them into a carrier bag she'd stuffed inside her pocket. Her secret was safe.

She was thankful that she had wrapped up warm in her black knee-length coat. Winter was fast approaching and the chilling wind was growing stronger. Her coat billowed behind her as she approached the clearing, the thick rubber soles of her heavy boots crunching the leaves and twigs beneath her as she emerged into the opening of the woods.

'Good evening,' the old lady walking a dog nodded to her as she passed. Winny didn't respond, but she did hear the old lady turn to her husband once they were a little further away and whisper: 'That's the girl who thinks she's a bat. She wants twenty-four-seven care, she does!'

Winny grumbled to herself in silence. She *was* a bat. She'd show them. Very soon.

She spent ten minutes wandering around the deserted woods, glancing up at the trees and studying their branches. She needed one that was tall but one that also had some branches low down that she could reach onto to pull herself up. Eventually, she found the perfect one.

Winny had never really been any good at climbing, but she pulled her black gloves onto her hands, slung the carrier bag onto her arm, and grabbed onto the lowest branch.

As she gripped onto it, she managed to scramble her way up the trunk by using the soles of her boots to provide her with enough force to swing herself onto the first branch. It was exhausting work, but she told herself not to look up, not to consider how much further she still had to climb, but to simply keep going.

Puffing and panting her way up the tree, Winny finally decided to stop once she was about halfway up. The branches were starting to thin out and she wasn't sure it would be wise to go any higher. Perching with her hands clasped around the branch on which she now sat, she glanced down beneath her for the first time since setting off on her journey up the tree. The ground was much further away than she had anticipated, the oranges and browns and reds of the leaves that coated the ground blending into one autumnal blur.

She felt woozy. Her stomach lurched. Just look forward, she told herself. This was what she had been waiting for; she couldn't let a simple little thing like a fear of heights stop her. Besides, bats weren't afraid of heights, were they? That would be silly.

Winny pulled the wings out of the carrier bag and straightened them out. Each wing was almost a metre in length, made from a combination of black nylon and faux leathers that had been sewn and shaped together. She had affixed two strips of elastic to the rods that ran down the middle, which she now slipped over her arms.

With the wings strapped behind her, she was no longer able to sit down. Steadying herself with a palm pressed against the trunk of the tree, she manoeuvred herself into a standing position. The wings were not as heavy as she had expected. That would make it much easier for her to glide across the sky as the wind would surely be able to carry them much easier if they weren't laden with heavy materials.

Shuffling a little further across the branch, holding onto the one above her for balance, Winny concentrated on her desired sensation of soaring freely among the clouds, whipping in and out of the trees, and swooping low to the ground before zooming back up. Away from the earth. Away from people. Away from the pain of being trapped in a life amongst a species that did not understand her.

Taking a deep breath, Winny spread an arm out, stretching out the left wing as she did so. The breeze tickled against the fabric as it longed to catch itself inside the wing. This was it. She was ready.

As quick as a flash, Winny stretched out her other arm, toppling only for a moment before she bent her legs and leapt from the branch. For a few slight seconds, she felt weightless as she seemed to hover in the air. She straightened her torso, her face forward, with the wings outstretched and majestic behind her. She was a dark shape in the night sky, ready to complete her physical transformation as she glided like the true bat she was.

And then the wind let go of her wings. In all happened so quickly that Winny didn't have any time to take in what was happening. She tumbled through the sky, colliding with branches as her body twisted and turned at a rapid rate as she hurtled towards the ground. The only sound she could emit was a high yelp not dissimilar to the squeak of a distressed vampire bat.

She landed in a heap at the base of the tree. Her legs were buckled. Her arms were bent. A pool of blood began to form where her head had whacked against the base of the tree trunk. But she could not smell the metallic tinge of her own crimson liquid as it seeped into the leaves and oozed over her black clothing. She could not feel the breaks in her bones or hear with bat-like acuteness the running feet that sped in her direction to find out what had caused such a frightening, deafening wail.

If Winny were to ever awaken again, she would have coped with the broken bones and cuts and bruises. She would have dealt with the unwanted attention and constant visits to the hospital. What she would have found unbearable, however, was that her wings – the very essence of her nature as a vampire bat – had not survived the fall. They had crumpled up beneath her, torn and ripped and bent out of shape. The metal rods jutted out at unnatural angles, and the elastic straps no longer clung to her body.

Winny had been convinced she was a bat, determined to live like a bat. She just needed to transform her exterior so that it could work in harmony with her internal emotions. However, Winny's mental state could never have worked alongside her physical surroundings. She would live as neither human nor bat. She would never have her wings to fly.

Isadora

Ludibrium Toys was situated between a patisserie deli and a retail store selling cheap imitation sports shoes. There was nothing unusual about the high street itself, offering the usual array of designer retailers, cheap alternatives, and more eateries than one could ever be bothered to count. All of the shops kept regular opening hours, and Mr Ludibrium's toy shop was no different. He would pull up the shutters first thing in the morning to reveal a small display in the old Victorian bay window, welcoming in a steady flow of customers – some new faces, others regular – before closing up the shop at the end of the day to head home.

Not that Mr Ludibrium had far to walk. His single-bedroomed apartment – a petite space, but not too cramped for the old man's needs – was above the shop, accessed by a staircase that was tucked away in the storeroom at the back, out of the sight of customers.

Every evening, the shopkeeper would carry out the same routine: after he had locked the door, releasing the day's final satisfying sound of the jingling bell that had been hanging above the entrance for many decades, Mr Ludibrium would ascend the stairs to his home, enjoy a brief supper of toast and marmalade, or buttered crumpets if he had had a particularly successful day, before heading into his workshop.

His workshop was a cluttered space filled with bits of wood, pots of paint, and odds and ends that would eventually become the finishing touches of Mr Ludibrium's latest project. Although the contents of the table from which he worked on his latest creation would change from one week to the next, the room looked little different to Mr Ludibrium's eyes as it did when his father used to command the space, and his father before him too. For three generations, since the dawn of the twentieth century, the Ludibriums had each in turn worked into the night to perfect their artwork and ensure that their hand-crafted toys were expertly finished and ready to find a home with whichever lucky boy or girl it was destined to belong to.

On this particular evening, just as the October dusk was beginning to creep in, Mr Ludibrium shuffled into his workshop and closed the door behind him, firmly pushing his palm against it to ensure that it was securely closed. He did so on this evening, despite the fact that he lived alone with nobody around to disturb him. It was part of his nightly routine before he settled down in his chair in the windowless room.

Mr Ludibrium sniffed and smiled down at the toy that lay in front of him. He had been working on this particular china doll for a while now, knowing that it would be an intense and time-consuming project, but it was almost finished. He was completely aware that the department store down the road – into which he only ever entered when he absolutely had to, which was seldom – sold such dolls by the shelf load, and that his humble little toy shop would never be able to compete with such volume.

He also knew, however, that no love had gone into the mass-produced creation of those bulk-stacked toys. They had been welded together by machine, stuffed into boxes and shipped off without a second consideration for the children who would soon be cherishing the toys as their very own. Mr Ludibrium shook his head at the thought, picked up a nearby paintbrush, and dipped it into a crimson red pool.

People had forgotten the innocence of childhood. That was the problem today, Mr Ludibrium thought as he began painting dainty blood-red lips beneath the doll's porcelain nose. The customers who came into his shop were those who still had fond memories of that special toy they had loved in their infancy. Many still treasured their childhood favourites, with some even bringing in their paint-chipped boats and bedraggled ragdolls and saggy stuffed animals for Mr Ludibrium to admire. He always loved seeing these old toys still being shown the love and care they deserved, particularly if they had been the work of his ancestors. Each toy made by the Ludibrium hand was finished off with a small Ludibrium stamp, a mark of pride for the family business. Where was the pride in those bulk-made toys?

The toymaker added faint eyebrows above the hollows of the doll's eyes to match her fair curls, before reaching into a small wooden box at the back of the table. Out of that box he pulled out two bright blue marble spheres and, applying a little strong adhesive to the sockets, pressed them firmly into the hollows beneath the doll's eyelashes.

'There, now! Welcome to the world, little one!' he declared as he lifted the doll up, careful not to tip her too far forward while her eyes were still setting. 'By morning, you'll be ready to go to your new home. I'll make sure I find a nice child to look after you,' he added before setting the doll back down onto the table, propping her up against the wall so that she could sit up and observe her surroundings.

'We need to name you though, don't we? Well now, let's see. What would suit you?'

Mr Ludibrium studied the doll's image. Her white round face was finished with two dusty pink rosy cheeks, soft brown curls hanging down either side of her face. Her cloth body was protected by a white cotton dress and red velvet coat, with silk white bloomers and matching socks to keep her warm. On her feet, a pair of suede black shoes completed her look.

'I know, we'll call you Isadora. That was my great grandmother's name. I think it suits you, wouldn't you agree?'

Satisfied with his decision, Mr Ludibrium pulled his weary bones out of his chair and shuffled towards the door. Before leaving the room for the night, he turned back to the doll and smiled. Just as he had been taught by his father as a boy, hard work always paid off. This unique creation was much more rewarding, he knew, than all of those other cloned dolls that were out there. 'You're very pretty, and there's only one of you. That makes you very special,' Mr Ludibrium said with genuine delight. He flicked the light switch to leave the room in darkness, before finishing: 'You're going to make somebody very happy indeed, Isadora. You're one of a kind.'

It was Emma's special day. She was turning six years old, and, best of all, it was a Saturday, which meant she didn't have to go to school.

'Mummy! Mummy! Mummy!' she yelled as she raced down the stairs, her dressing gown tightly wrapped around her little body to keep out the morning chill.

'Happy birthday, sleepy head! Is my birthday princess ready for her breakfast?'

Mrs Welch lifted Emma onto her knee. She sipped at her coffee before stroking her daughter's long blonde hair.

'Well now, who's this big girl?' Mr Welch gasped as he entered the room with a grin, his hands thrown out in front of him in mock confusion. 'You're not Emma! Where's my little girl gone?'

'Da-ad!' Emma protested. 'It's me! I'm just grown up now!'

'Yes you are, my big birthday girl. You're almost an adult now! Hey, don't you think it's time you started looking for a job? I know a guy who could fix you up with a paper round...'

Emma burst into giggles as her father lent forward to tickle her waist. Mrs Welch took the opportunity to reach down beside her while Emma wasn't looking to bring up a parcel that had been concealed behind the dining chair. She set it down on the table to display the shiny purple wrapping paper finished off with a silver bow.

'Oh wow!' Emma exclaimed as she slid off her mother's knee. 'Can I open it now? Can I, can I?'

'Of course you can! Happy birthday, my darling.' Mrs Welch kissed the top of her head as Emma tore into the present.

Once the clean white box was uncovered, Emma gingerly pulled the lid off the top and peered inside. Her eyes widened in delight.

'Could it be true? Has Emma Welch finally been rendered speechless?' Mr Welch teased.

True enough, Emma said nothing. Instead, she reached into the box, carefully tucking her hands around the doll's back to lift her out.

'She's beautiful,' she managed to whisper as she cradled the china doll in her arms. 'What's her name?'

'The man in the toy shop said she was called Isadora,' Mrs Welch explained. 'But I'm sure you could call her whatever you want to. She's your very own baby doll, after all. Just what you asked for, isn't it?'

Emma shook her head. 'I don't want to change her name. She's perfect. Thank you, Mummy. Thank you, Daddy.' She looked up at her parents with a genuine watery-eyed gratitude for her special present. She may not have known the labour that went into the doll's birth, but Emma was one little girl who could appreciate its unique beauty.

'Now, don't you think we should have some breakfast? You've got a big day ahead of you, and it won't be long before your party guests arrive!' Mrs Welch reminded her.

Emma, with her stomach suddenly rumbling at the thought of food, placed Isadora back into her box. 'You can enjoy a nice nap, Isadora. I'll play with you soon, I promise. We're going to be the best of friends. I just know it!'

Isadora's nap lasted all day and into the evening while Emma was busy playing musical statues, gulping down bowls of jelly, and enjoying a burger in her favourite restaurant with her parents. By the time she had cleaned her teeth and climbed into bed, Emma was exhausted.

She was quietly singing a nursery rhyme to herself in the dark while she waited for her mother to come and tuck her in. She had had a wonderful day. Yes, she decided, being six years old was much better than being five. She hugged Isadora tightly to her chest and smiled.

When Mrs Welch came into Emma's bedroom to say goodnight, she raised an eyebrow at the doll. 'I'm not sure either of you will be particularly comfortable sharing a bed. Why don't we let Isadora sit here?' she suggested as she slid the doll out from Emma's grasp and placed her instead on the chair beside Emma's bed.

Emma nodded as she admired Isadora's vacant expression. 'Won't she be lonely?'

'Oh no. She'll be sound asleep all night, just like you will be. And then in the morning she'll be nice and refreshed to play with you. Now, why don't you lie down so you can both fall fast asleep? You must be tired after the day you've had!' Emma nodded. 'Did you have fun?'

'Yes!' Emma replied a little too energetically.

'Good! Well, settle down now.' Mrs Welch kissed her forehead and pulled the blanket up around Emma's shoulders. 'Goodnight. Sleep tight. Don't let the bed bugs bite!'

Mrs Welch left the door open to allow a little light from the hallway drift into the room as Emma closed her eyes. Moments later, she was sound asleep, and the room fell into silence.

It was at that moment that Isadora blinked.

She turned her head left and then right, glancing around her to take in the room. Apart from that annoying child with the screeching voice and sickeningly cute giggle, there was nobody else in the room. She was safe.

Shuffling her bottom forward, her silk bloomers sliding across the plastic surface, Isadora shifted her weight until she was perched on the ledge of the chair. With a single push, she leapt – as much as a doll without kneecaps could leap – the short distance from the chair and down onto the carpet, landing with a soft thud.

With a rush of panic, she glanced at her limbs, straining her eyes in the darkness to make sure there were no cracks. The last thing she needed was a broken arm.

Had she been able to open her mouth, she would have exhaled with relief. No harm done. She was going to have to be extra careful though. Wasn't that what the child's mother had said to her? Isadora was a fragile doll, and she had to be treated delicately.

Delicate, my silk-covered arse! Isadora thought to herself as she marched across the carpet towards the bedroom door, her movements surprisingly agile for one with straight legs. She paused to make sure nobody was watching, before sliding out of the room. Faint whispers came from the room down the hall. Isadora pretty sure she recognised the voices as those belonging to the child's parents, which meant only one thing: downstairs was deserted.

Time to put my plan into action and escape this joint!

Out of sight, Isadora crept towards the top of the stairs. She glanced down to the bottom. They looked much steeper than she had anticipated. Steadying herself, she took a step, using the banister to steer her movements. After a brief exertion, Isadora had finally made it. She had climbed down the first step.

Only twenty-nine more to go.

What use are these bloody shoes?! she grumped to herself. *There's hardly any material here. How are these supposed to protect my feet?!* The old man – that fool who had dressed her up in these hideous clothes – had carried her down to the shelf where all the other dolls were. *Those stupid, silent, good-for-nothing lumps of porcelain.* And since Emma had carried her everywhere today too, Isadora was finding out only now how difficult it was to walk with porcelain feet and unsupportive footwear.

This only made her more infuriated. More determined to set herself free from the intolerable clutches of unbearable childlike fun.

Panting behind her sealed mouth, Isadora finally made it to the bottom step. She took a moment to compose herself as she tried to remember which way the front door was. If she could only find that, and somehow manage to slip outside, she would be able to live her life as she pleased. She could explore the wide world as she intended, instead of remaining trapped with this deplorable family.

Moving about was tiring work when you were only a foot tall. Isadora stomped her way around the downstairs of the family home, growing frustrated as she found herself wandering into the living room on three separate occasions after emerging from the hallway.

Where is the stupid bloody door?! She kicked the wall in anger. *Ouch!* A shooting pain ran up her leg. Isadora pulled down her sock to inspect the damage: a hairline crack now made its way from her heel to the top of her porcelain leg.

Oh shit! Well, that's not going to make this any easier.

If she wanted to get out before anybody woke up, she was going to have to act fast. A fractured leg was going to stall her.

With as much gusto as she could summon, Isadora stamped into the next room. She'd not been in the kitchen since that morning when the child released her from her suffocating prison. She still couldn't see the front door, but at least she was making progress.

Just as she was about to leave the room and try another one, something caught Isadora's eye. A street lamp outside cast its light in through the kitchen window, reflecting on the surface of the worktop. And on that worktop, glistening beneath the lamplight, was the knife that had been used to cut the child's birthday cake earlier that day.

Suddenly an idea began to form in Isadora's mind.

Oh, I've been such an idiot! Why would I choose to go into the cold outdoors when I could just claim this home as my own? I can be such a fool sometimes! Gah!

19

It seemed like the perfect solution now that Isadora had thought of it. There was only one problem though.

How am I going to reach the knife?

The doll glanced around her, searching for a solution. She could climb up onto the chair, then lift herself onto the table. It might work. But if she fell... No, it wasn't worth the risk. Besides, it would take her too long. She needed a better plan.

It took Isadora another minute as she slumped against the table leg, her round chin resting in her hand, to notice the dish cloth that was draped over the back of the chair.

That's it!

Isadora stretched her arm up to pull down the cloth. She was too small. She couldn't reach.

It was no use. She was going to have to climb.

And climb she did. She clambered onto the leg of the chair, lifting her entire body weight up until she could grab onto the seat. Pulling herself upright, she stretched her hand out.

Almost...almost there...Nearly...Got it!

The dish cloth fell down to the ground. Isadora slid down the chair leg after it, and scooped it up. Now all she had to do was hope that the rest of her new plan worked. It was always a risk to deviate from one's original strategy, but Isadora had to make this work.

It was quite simple, really. All she had to do was grip tightly onto one end of the dish cloth, and fling it in the direction of the knife. It was close enough to the edge of the worktop – *what kind of idiotic parents leave a kitchen knife within reach of little people?* - and coax it down towards her.

Isadora whirled the dish cloth over her head and cast it forward.

Missed.

She tried again.

Missed.

Each time, it narrowly avoided the knife. It was too lightweight. It needed something to guide it.

Isadora glanced down. Realised what she had to do.

You may be useless as a shoe, she thought as she untied a flimsy shoelace, *but you won't let me down as a catapult, will you?*

Now with one exposed foot, Isadora tied one end of the dish cloth into a knot around the shoe. She lifted it up and down, testing its weight. *Much better.*

She swung the weighted dish cloth around her head a few times to develop momentum, and flung it forward with all her might.

Even Isadora could hardly believe that it had worked as she watched the shoe knock into the knife. It tumbled to the ground, clattering on the wooden flooring.

Shit!

Isadora froze, her eyes shooting sideways in the direction of the stairs. If she had any breath to hold, she would have done so then, as she listened for any sounds of movement from upstairs. But nobody seemed to have stirred.

Phew!

Isadora paused for only a moment before reaching down for the knife. The handle was large and heavy, and fit awkwardly in the

21

palm of her unopposable hand, but she was still able to grip onto it, and that was the main thing. Now she just had to find a way to carry both the knife and herself upstairs. It was now or never though, and she knew that. Shuffling her way through the kitchen, her porcelain toes clacking against the hard flooring, she wasn't going to let anything get in the way of her freedom. She would be a trapped toy no more.

Spurred by the sound of the ticking clock that echoed from the hallway, Isadora fought her way back up the stairs. She had no choice but to reach the knife up onto the next step before pulling her own body onto it, picking the knife back up, and repeating the process for each of the thirty steps, but eventually she made it.

This better be worth it, she thought as she regained her composure. She studied the situation for a moment, working out how best to approach it.

The parents. Definitely the parents first. Then nobody can save the child.

Satisfied that she had made the right decision, Isadora crept through to the bedroom at the end of the corridor. The vibrating snores that floated down to the ground ensured Isadora that she was safe to throw the knife up onto the bed without being seen, before clambering up after it, using the bedsheet to lift herself up.

Her eyes wide and gleaming, she stood over the adult humans with the knife wielded in both hands. There was no sign of movement from either of them. Everything was perfect.

Take that, *you son of a bitch!*

Without any further hesitation, Isadora plummeted the knife down through the air and struck it straight into Mr Welch's neck.

Blood spurted out, drenching the white bedsheet and splashing across Mrs Welch's cheek.

The sudden wetness that had struck her face caused Mrs Welch to bolt awake. She screamed as she first noticed Isadora's own blood-speckled face inches from her own. There was no time for her to notice the knife, however, as Isadora released an inaudible scream of her own, and plunged it through Mrs Welch's breast and straight into her heart. The doll continued to stab the knife back and forth until Mrs Welch's body slumped against the pillow.

Well then. That wasn't too difficult.

Only the child to go now.

Fuelled by a new energy that Isadora could not have anticipated, she hopped off the bed, sliding down the blood-soaked bedcover, and tottled her way into Emma's bedroom. The child, although having stirred at the sound of her mother's final cry for help, had not fully awakened. Her eyelids fluttered as she detected movement in the room.

Sleepily, she opened an eye and squinted in the dark. Whatever the child had expected to find, she never would have imagined seeing her birthday gift standing at the bottom of her bed, her knife-laden hands clasped behind her back.

'Isadora? What are you doing?' To anybody else, it would have seemed like a peculiar question, but in her half-dazed state it was a perfectly natural thing for Emma to ask her doll.

Hello, little girl. We're going to play a game now. You like games, don't you?

Emma, unable to hear the voice inside Isadora's head, didn't respond. It didn't matter to Isadora. Regardless of whether or not the child understood what was about to happen, her fate would still be the same.

It's a little game I like to call 'let's see how long it takes for the child to die'. Would you like to play, little girl?

Isadora took a few steps closer to Emma, who was slowly coming round from sleep.

'I...I don't understand...'

There was no time for Emma to finish expressing her confusion. Isadora, sensing that the child would soon be fully awake and able to run from her, jumped forward, brandishing the knife.

Emma screamed with a satisfying yelp as Isadora collided into her chest. The knife struck Emma just below the ribs as crimson pools began to form on the surface of her pyjamas. Isadora plunged the knife into her stomach, into her arms, anywhere she could find as the girl frantically thrashed about, crying out for her mother.

Mummy can't save you now, brat!

One final strike just above her collarbone, and Emma's small body quivered before falling limp and lifeless.

Isadora dropped the knife and stepped back to admire her work. The parents were dead. The child was dead. Isadora was free.

How cute she looks, she thought as she admired Emma's pale complexion. Her blonde hair was stained and matted with her own blood. It was only considerate of Isadora to smooth it out across the pillow for the child. With her porcelain fist, she nudged Emma's face so that her head turned sideways. If it wasn't for the blood that surrounded her, anybody would think she was sleeping.

And really, that's all she was doing. An everlasting, eternal sleep.

And while the child slept, Isadora was free to live the life that she deserved. The hard work was over. Now she could relax.

Before sliding back down onto the floor to claim her territory, Isadora took one last look at Emma. Something wasn't right. She looked so sad. Isadora couldn't have that. Leaning forward, she reached out her hand towards Emma's tiny, parted lips, and pushed at either side until it looked like she was smiling. She had been a happy child. That was evident as she had screeched and laughed and tormented Isadora's poor ears. There was no reason why she shouldn't be happy in death either.

She looked so peaceful, Isadora thought. Yes, executing her new plan had exerted her, and Isadora was now so exhausted that she was in desperate need for a nap. Before tumbling onto the floor to find somewhere to rest her head, Isadora smoothed down the child's hair one final time, and admired the punctures of her handiwork with her permanent, painted smile.

Memento Mori

'Come on, it'll be fun!'

'I don't want to. Besides, don't you need one of those board things for that?'

'A Ouija board? No, not necessarily. We just need to call out to them. They'll be able to hear us. I've read up about these things. Trust me.'

'I do trust you. I just don't exactly like the idea of spending too much time in a graveyard. They give me the creeps.'

'I agree with Cass. I don't think we should do it either, Sarah.'

'What? You were all up for this earlier, Ben!'

'I know, but now that it's starting to get dark it seems a bit more...I don't know. Real, I guess.'

'Tell you what. Why don't we head up there anyway, and if after ten minutes neither of you feel comfortable, we can leave. It's not as if we have anything better to do tonight.'

'Fine. But you have to promise.'

'I do promise. Cass?'

'Alright, but you better mean it when you say ten minutes. I'm not staying any longer than that.'

And so, if only to keep Sarah happy, Cass and Ben trudged behind her as they headed for her car to drive up the bank towards the graveyard. The moon was shining brightly above them, casting a faint silver glow onto the headstones as they clambered over the locked gate. Fifteen minutes later, after Sarah refused to leave so soon, and with the others having little choice but to wait for her to unlock the car, they found themselves huddling close for warmth by a cluster of nineteenth-century graves. Two minutes after, once Sarah began to tease the others with unintelligible mutterings, she had raised the dead.

Sarah didn't know what she found more surprising: the fact that her juvenile fun-and-games chanting had worked, having only found the chants on some random website after searching around for a laugh; the fact that only a few bodies had emerged from a seemingly random selection of graves; or the fact that these living dead corpses had slumped straight by them without so much as a glance in their direction.

Yes, for these zombies – was there a more cliché way of describing them? – appeared to have no interest in Sarah, Ben, and Cass.

With Sarah's eyes tightly shut during her recital, it had been Cass who had noticed the first hand shoot up through the earth, sending loose soil spraying across the headstone. As one might expect her to react, she had shrieked, alerting the others just in time for them to see several other decaying limbs pop up through the ground.

There wasn't any time for Ben and Cass to express their fury at Sarah as they observed with wide eyes the bodies pulling and heaving their rotten corpses out of their coffins.

Their movements were sluggish, but the gang took no chances. Fuelled by his own mixture of fear and disbelief, Ben threw the heel of his trainer against the padlocked gate. A few more kicks in rapid succession, and the gate swung open.

'Oh, that's just fantastic, Ben! Now they'll be able to get out!' Cass exclaimed.

'I'm sorry, but I didn't fancy our chances of climbing back over that stupid fence. It would have taken too long and—'

But even as the words left his mouth, he knew it was an irrelevant point. Seven zombies trundled in the direction of the open gate, which Sarah, Ben, and Cass could now watch from a safer distance as they paused to regain their bearings on the other side of the road.

The bodies shuffled along, appearing dazed and groggy as if having recently awoken from a long nap.

'Where are they going?' Sarah, who had until this point remained uncharacteristically speechless, asked with a raised eyebrow as they watched them file out of the cemetery. They dispersed at their own paces as they began meandering their way down the hill in the direction of the town.

'Don't ask me!' Cass protested. 'This was your doing!'

'Oh, come on. It's not as if I actually thought it was going to work. It was just supposed to be a bit of a laugh, you know? A bit of fun!'

'Yeah, well I don't hear anybody laughing. You've just unleashed that *bit of fun* on the whole town!'

'I hardly think they're going to do any damage. Look how slowly they're moving!'

'You're such a fool.'

'Ladies, please! This isn't the time for bickering,' Ben intervened. 'Besides, I think Sarah may have a point. Maybe they won't do any harm. I mean, they completely ignored us, didn't they? Surely if they had wanted to savage us they would have done?'

'Yeah, that was weird,' Cass admitted. 'So what do they want?'

'I've no idea. But I do think you're acting far too calmly about this, Ben,' Sarah added.

'I reckon we should follow them.'

'Are you mad? No way am I going after them! This is Sarah's mess, Ben—'

'Gee, thanks for the support.'

'Regardless of whose fault this is or isn't—'

'It's Sarah's.'

'—we need to do something. I say we follow them at a safe distance, and at least find out where they're heading.'

'And how are we going to explain a pack of zombies wandering through the town?'

'It's Halloween, Cass. They'll fit right in!'

Ben was right. In the increasing darkness of the evening, nobody seemed to flinch as the seven bedraggled zombies crept down the hill one by one.

'Can't they see the corpses are falling apart?' Cass asked. 'That one's only got one arm, and his head's practically falling off!' she added with a shudder.

'They probably think it's just really convincing make-up. You know how advanced costumes can be these days.'

'Look!' Sarah interrupted. She pointed discreetly to a house

29

over the road just in time to see one of the zombies trudge inside.

'Let's go!'

By the time they had made it to the other side and ducked into the garden to peer through the front window, the corpse was slowly entering the living room. It had once been the healthy body of a dark-haired man in his mid-forties. He had been buried in a navy suit, which at one point would have been an elegant tailored fit but now hung loose around his depleting frame. Neither suit nor corpse had fared well during the few years they had spent underground.

'What's he doing?' Cass whispered as they watched the zombie shuffle in the direction of the armchair that was positioned in front of a television.

The man sitting enjoying a late-night Bela Lugosi marathon was not quick enough to notice the intruder. Without warning, the zombie reached out his hands from behind the chair, and clasped them tightly around the man's throat. He squeezed his bony fingers together until the man's body fell limp.

It was like watching a live silent horror film.

'I thought you said they weren't dangerous!' Cass stammered.

'I think I might have been mistaken. Quick, let's get out of here.'

They had barely managed to flee from the garden when the zombie emerged from the house. His expression remained vacant as he started back up the hill as if nothing had happened.

'Is he heading back into the graveyard?' Cass's eyes flitted back and forth in confusion.

'It certainly looks like it. Come on, let's follow him.'

'What about the others?'

Ben glanced back down the hill, and swiftly counted all six of the remaining zombies. They were all in sight, having made it little further down the road with their slow movements. They mingled among the trick-or-treaters without attracting any attention. They still had some time.

'We'll only be a minute. The graveyard's just there, so it won't take this guy here very long to reach it.'

And true enough, they were soon standing again in the gateway of the graveyard, just in time to see the corpse sliding back into his plot, the earth crumbling back down on top of him.

'Do we know who it is? Er, was?' Cass asked.

Ben took a few steps closer, and, using the light from his mobile phone as a torch, squinted at the inscription on the headstone.

'Carlton Samuel Davidson,' he read out loud. 'Died two years ago. Never heard of him. You guys?'

'I don't recognise the name.'

'Nope, me neither. Do you reckon he'll stay in there now?' Sarah asked with a surprising calm. The last thing any of them needed was to become too comfortable with the situation. They were dealing with zombies, after all, and they had seen enough horror films to know that that was never a good thing.

'I hope so,' Ben replied, 'as I really think we should go and find the others now.' He took a deep breath before slowly releasing the air. 'Hey, don't look at me like that, Cass. I know it's scary, but...let's just think of it an as adventure. Maybe it won't be so bad.

Hey, you never know. It could be quite fun! Certainly more interesting than the nothing we'd had planned for this evening anyway.'

'See, I bet you're glad I had the idea now, aren't you?'

Cass simply glared at Sarah as they left the graveyard and headed in search of the remaining zombies.

The next body they came across must have been only recently buried; her skin was a little sallow and gaunt, but her features were still defined, and her hair was still its natural rich black as it tumbled down her back towards her waist. She was slender and elegant, dressed in an expensive red dress and matching stiletto heels. They clacked softly against the pavement as she shuffled along.

The gang followed this zombie through several streets, remaining at a reasonable distance behind her out of necessary precaution.

'Where's she going now?' Cass whined as they watched the zombie turn yet another corner. A group of young children dressed as witches and wizards zoomed past them. One or two turned to look at the zombie, but nobody paid her much attention beyond that. If anything, it was Sarah, Ben, and Cass who looked more out of place in their plain clothes and apparent lack of Halloween spirit.

Before anybody could reply to Cass, the female zombie pushed open a rickety garden gate and headed for the main door of the house. They had meandered into a rougher part of town now, and nobody particularly enjoyed being there, but this zombie didn't seem phased by any of it. They watched as she reached down, her near-perfect body creaking slightly as she felt under the doormat. When she stood up again, she held onto something in her hand.

'What is it?' Sarah asked.

'I could be mistaken, but I think it's a key.'

Sure enough, a second later the zombie was fitting the key into the lock of the door. She turned it and pushed the door open, before entering the house.

The trio hurried along the path to catch up with her, but decided it wasn't worth crossing over the threshold onto the property. They had no idea who lived here, but they didn't particularly wish to find out either.

'Why's she taking so long?'

'It's only been a few minutes, Cass, and she doesn't exactly move very fast. Besides, we don't know what she's doing.'

'Maybe she'll never come back out. What if we're wasting our time?'

Almost as soon as Cass had finished her protest, a faint but definite scream floated out of the upstairs window.

'What was that?!'

'It sounded like a man.'

'Should we help him? Should we call somebody?'

'And tell them what? That you summoned up a bunch of zombies and now they're going around attacking people at random?'

Sarah had no response for that.

'Look, here she comes!'

They hid behind a hedge as the zombie trudged down the

stairs. She was still fresh enough to still have all of her brain inside her skull, enabling her to shut the door behind her before leaving the garden.

'Is that...blood on her hands?'

Ben simply nodded.

'Oh my God! He's dead too, isn't he?' Cass whimpered with a glance up to the bedroom window.

'I would put money on it. Come on, we can't lose her.'

Sarah and Cass closely followed behind Ben as they kept up with the corpse. She moved a little more quickly now, as if killing that man, whatever her reason, had provided her with some sort of energy. Ten minutes and several streets later, they had returned to the graveyard. Just as they had observed with the first zombie, this one slid back into her coffin, blood and mud streaking her milky white arms as she disappeared out of sight.

'She can't have been buried long. No way.'

'According to her headstone, she was buried this year.' Ben suddenly had an idea. He whipped his phone out of his pocket and began punching in letters.

'What are you doing?'

'I'm typing in her name. If she was only buried recently then it's possible there's some sort of news story or obituary online that could give us more information. Aha! Here's something. It says that Sandra Leroy died on September thirtieth. Oh wow!'

'What?'

'Well, it says in this article that she had died after she had cut her own wrists, but that her family don't believe she would ever have committed suicide. She was from a wealthy part of town too, so whoever owned that house she went into, it wasn't hers.'

'You mean her family think she was murdered?'

'According to this article.'

'What about the other guy? That Carlton whatshisname?'

Ben searched for his details, and instantly pulled up a list of results.

'You'll never believe this.'

'What?'

'Carlton Samuel Davidson, forty-two, was found in the middle of the motorway after having been the victim of a hit-and-run. The driver of the vehicle, which turned out to be stolen, was never found after the car was abandoned nearby.'

'He was murdered too.'

'Yes. Well, manslaughter perhaps. But he was still killed by somebody else.'

'Do you think...'

'What, Sarah?'

'Oh, I don't know. It's a stupid thought, really.'

Cass rolled her eyes. 'We're out chasing zombies in the middle of the night. I don't think *stupid* really comes into play here.'

'Fair point. Well, what if these zombies have gone after their killers? Maybe that's why they completely ignored us, and are seemingly oblivious to everybody else they're passing on the streets.'

'You mean like unfinished business?' Ben asked, suddenly very interested in this theory.

'I guess so, yes.'

'Sarah, you may just be onto something.' Ben glanced back at his phone before shoving it into his pocket. 'It's almost ten o'clock. There are still five zombies out there. I don't know about you guys, but I suddenly feel really into this now!'

'You're insane, Ben. They're *zombies*. Corpses! Dead people!'

Ben put an arm around Cass's shoulder. 'I know that, Cass, but they're not going to hurt us, are they? If Sarah's right - and I think she might just be – then they're only after certain people. And since I'm assuming none of us has ever killed anybody before, we should be safe. Still, it's our responsibility to make sure they all return to where they belong. What do you say, Cass? Will you help me and Sarah?'

'I really don't—'

'Please, Cass.' It was Sarah who spoke this time, with a genuine smile that suggested she needed her best friend right now.

Cass sighed. 'Oh, alright. But this better not take long.'

Unfortunately, it did take long. The first challenge was to find the other zombies. And then, with their movements still deathly slow, it wasn't exactly a quick process of chasing them back up to the graveyard before beginning all over again. It was laborious and lengthy, but they all knew it had to be done.

It was fortunate that two of the bodies had made their way to adjacent streets, allowing Cass and Sarah to follow one and Ben to observe the other. As they had expected, one of the zombies had been the victim of a brutal murder, only a few decades back, but the culprit had been found not guilty. The other zombie, however, was little more than a walking bag of bones, thankfully draped in a large coat so that nobody could see just how realistic he looked as a skeleton. He had been buried at the back of the graveyard over forty years ago; there was nothing on the internet about his death, nor his life.

'How can his killer even still be alive?!'

'Perhaps he was murdered by somebody much younger that he was.'

'Do you think he's killed whoever it was then?' Cass asked as they followed the skeleton back up the hill, having found him too late to witness his act.

'I've no idea, Cass. I honestly think I'd rather not know.'

With four zombies down, there were only three left to find. It was nearing midnight now, and their energies were weakening, so it was quite a relief when they found the fifth body slumping up the hill just as they were about to leave the graveyard again.

'Well, that's convenient,' Sarah muttered.

'It's quite poetic, don't you think?' Ben suddenly said.

'What? Murdering the person that stole your life from you?' Cass shrugged. 'I can think of more romantic things to write about.'

'Still. Justice must be found. Come on, there's only two left now. And I really need sleep, so the quicker we get moving, the sooner we can put a lid on this.'

The streets were deserted now, meaning the gang didn't have to be too careful about attracting the wrong sort of attention. It also meant that they were able to run around without being seen, making their search much quicker than before.

Their penultimate zombie, it turned out, was an elderly lady both Sarah and Cass had known since they were children. They found Mrs Shackle just two streets away from their old nursery school, sliding her way into her old home where her widowed husband still lived.

'I thought she died of severe food poisoning a few years ago? Dodgy fish or something, wasn't it?'

'I thought that too, but...Oh God, I can't look!'

Ben was the only person to see Mrs Shackle push Mr Shackle down the stairs. He tumbled with a whimper before landing in a heap at the bottom, snapping his neck as he fell.

'He's gone,' Ben explained as they walked and talked behind Mrs Shackle's shuffling corpse.

'I just can't believe Mr Shackle would do anything to harm his wife. He always seemed like such a kind man. What could he possibly gain from killing her?'

'Maybe he didn't do it on purpose?'

'It must be difficult to accidentally poison somebody,' Ben chipped in. 'Still, it looks like he got his comeuppance.'

'I don't know how you can be so blasé about this, Ben. A man just died!'

'No, Cass, a *monster* just died. We thought the zombies were the monsters, but they're not. They're the victims. It's about time people paid for their suffering.'

'Ben, you're talking crazy, do you know that?'

'Yes, well, I just don't like seeing criminals getting off lightly. How would you feel if somebody you loved was murdered? Wouldn't you want to see the killer suffer?'

Cass stopped in her tracks. 'Ben, what's going on?'

Ben halted. He rubbed his hands across his tired eyes. Sighed. 'My aunt was murdered when I was a child. A mugging gone wrong. Her killer was never caught. I've never mentioned it because I don't like talking about it, okay?'

'Oh, Ben. I'm so sorry. I had no idea.'

'Yeah, Ben. Me too. So that's why you were so set on making sure these zombies got back safely?'

A shrug. 'I suppose so.'

'And your aunt? Is she buried—?'

'Over on the other side of town. It's okay, she's not here. Thank goodness. I don't think I could bear to see her after all this time in the ground.' He shuddered, before pulling himself together. 'Anyway, come on. Let's drop Mrs Shackle off and then find our last body. Just one more to go now.'

It turned out that this last zombie was going to be the most difficult of them all.

'I know who she is!' Cass declared once they read the name above the remaining empty plot. 'Oh goodness, I can't believe this!'

'What? Who is it?'

'Do you remember little Lauren Lucie?'

'The girl who was molested? Sure I do. She...Oh God. She was murdered by her own father and buried beneath the floorboards for two years before anybody found her. That's who's left?'

Cass could do nothing but nod slowly.

'But her father was caught. He's in prison now, isn't he?'

'Then I guess that's where we're heading,' Ben suggested. 'Sarah, I think we better take your car. It's quite far from here.'

It was almost two o'clock in the morning when they parked outside of the prison. They clambered out of the car as silently as possible before glancing around.

'How are we supposed to find her?'

'I've no idea. I've never even been anywhere near here before.'

They spent a few minutes wandering the perimeter of the building. It wasn't the largest, but still big enough that they couldn't take it all in with one glance.

'How could she even get in? The wall runs all the way around.'

'Look over there!' Ben gestured towards the wall at the far side of the road. 'A person – or a zombie, I suppose – could easily climb up here if their feet were small enough to fit into these pockets. I bet a little girl could manage that no problem.'

'But she's only five. And dead.'

'Yeah, well, I guess revenge comes with a lot of internal strength,' Ben remarked.

Cass held out her hand for silence. 'Can you guys hear that?'

They listened. The sound of scratching grew louder until Cass was forced to look up.

'Oh my God!'

The small frame of a five-year-old girl dressed in a tattered summer dress was clambering over the wall, right above where they were standing. For a zombie, she moved surprisingly swiftly. She dropped onto the ground with a subtle thud, oblivious to the others, before tottling off down the road.

'Did—did you see her face?!' Cass gasped.

'Awful, isn't it?'

Her skin was taut against her skull but the scar than ran from her ear to the corner of her mouth was unmistakable. Even in death it served as a permanent reminder of the torture she had suffered. Her eyes were sunken and her bones were protruding through her lack of flesh. There was no expression about her, and yet she still managed to ooze sorrow. However, what had caused Cass's stomach to lurch the most was the streaks of blood that smothered her dainty pale lips. It was fresh and crimson, bubbling slightly between her teeth. In the morning, a prison warden would enter the cell of Mr Lucie to find an unexplainable tear in his neck where his dead daughter had bitten a huge chunk out of his flesh. It would be all over the news, and nobody except Sarah, Ben, and Cass would know the truth.

'It's just so heartbreaking. Oh God, I can't believe I'm feeling sorry for a zombie.'

'She was just a helpless little girl.'

'Right, come on then, you two. Sarah, let's head back up to the graveyard. You can drive slowly behind her, can't you? It's probably best if we don't let her out of our sight.' Sarah nodded, and the three of them set off to where their evening had begun.

*

'Okay, that's one, two, three, four, five, six, and...seven,' Ben counted after little Lauren Lucie dropped back down into her petite coffin. 'It's over. It's done. And,' he glanced at his watch, 'it's three o'clock in the morning. Will you two be alright getting home?'

'Of course. Do you want a lift?'

'No, it's alright. I'm only a two-minute walk from here, and after what we've seen tonight I think I can handle that!'

'Okay. I'll call you in the morning after we've all had some rest?'

Hugs were exchanged, and Sarah and Cass watched as Ben walked away from the graveyard and out of sight.

'He'll be okay, won't he?' Cass asked as they clambered back into Sarah's car.

'Of course he will be. For now, anyway. I don't know about you, but I have a feeling that whatever it is that's happened tonight hasn't really sunk in yet. And, Cass, I truly am sorry. If I'd had any idea that something like this was going to happen, I never would have—'

Cass found herself releasing a small, delirious laugh. 'Sarah, it's okay. I never thought it was going to work either. It's crazy. Insane. If it had been any other night, we probably would have had the town in hysterics. I suppose it's a blessing that it happened tonight.' A thought suddenly struck her. 'Hey, what do you think will happen when the bodies are discovered?'

'The ones the zombies killed? I've no idea,' Sarah replied as she pulled the car away from the graveyard. 'Mr Shackle just took a tumble. That won't seem too mysterious. As for the others though,

I wouldn't like to think. I guess we'll find out soon enough.'

As Sarah turned her head in Cass's direction to flash her friend a comforting smile, she had been unable to see the man stumbling out of the house on the other side of the road.

At least, he had been a living, breathing man the day previously. Now, however, he was a walking corpse.

As that first of the seven killers had died, a new zombie had been born. And that man, the murderer of Carlton Samuel Davidson, had only a few hours ago been strangled to death by his own victim.

And, as the trio had learned that evening, corpses who had been previously murdered had only one motive: to kill their own killer. And since Carlton Samuel Davidson was already dead and unkillable, this new zombie was going to have to find his revenge elsewhere.

After all, it was not only Carlton Samuel Davidson who was responsible for his death. It was the three students who had unleashed the corpses, and this new zombie knew them instinctively as Sarah, Ben, and Cass.

And now Sarah, Ben, and Cass were responsible for the murders of six other fresh corpses too, all of whom would soon be growing into their new rotting forms and heading off in search of their killers. The chain had begun, and the gang had no idea just how much danger they were in as these freshly unleashed corpses took to the streets of the town to hunt them down, tear them apart, and feast on their flesh until a new batch of zombies had been born.

Of Rat Hearts and Thunderstorms

As far as the life of a rat was concerned, Terence knew he had little to complain about. But it was not enough.

His family, the Fergusons, played with him every day. They fed him and watered him and made sure he always had soft, warm bedding in which he could curl up and sleep. Terence would sit calmly on the children's knees as they stroked his dark brown fur, accepting treats from their hands before enjoying a run around in his plastic exercise ball.

And all that was fine and dandy. Except there were twenty-four hours in a day, and his family could only spare him a small fraction of that time. For the rest of his existence, Terence was trapped behind the bars of the prison more commonly referred to as his cage.

Sure, when he was a baby, all fresh-whiskered and tiny squeaks, he loved exploring the three tiers of his own special home. He would run up the ladders and dive down the slide. He could snuggle up tightly inside the little plastic house in his very own nest. It was such a warm environment, and it was his very own.

But then Terence grew up, and he began to tire of the same surroundings. He started to wonder if there was more of the world to be explored. His family left the home every day; there had to be *something* else out there. How he longed to venture out and find out the truth.

But he was stuck. He was a big rat now, well fed with a thick, slithering tail; it would be impossible for him to squeeze out of those wretched bars. All he wanted was a little adventure. Was that too much to ask?

While Terence never gave up hope that he would one day be able to feel the sweet release of freedom, he knew that, every night after lights out, he would have to wait an entire day before he could stretch his legs and flex his whiskers again.

By this stage, Terence had been living with the Fergusons for over a year, and he had become accustomed to his routine. He knew when he would be able to exercise, knew when he would be handled and petted and played with. He had never been away from his family for more than a day. So when he saw them all heading out of the room with large cases and more bags than they could carry, he couldn't work out what was going on. They had never left him alone for too long before. Why would they need so much stuff? Where could they possibly all be going?

'Don't worry, Terence,' the youngest boy said as he bounded over to his cage. 'We'll only be gone two weeks. Mrs Potts from next door will come in every day to feed you.'

'Come on, Max. We're going to miss the flight if we don't get a move on!'

It was Mrs Ferguson. She sounded frantic as she bundled the family out of the house. The door closed behind them with a heavy thud.

Terence, with his nose pressed up against the cold bars of his cage, was all alone. Two weeks? What did that mean? And who was Mrs Potts?

Unsure of what he was supposed to do now, Terence slumped

down and sulked off to his little house to curl up and sleep it off. Maybe everything would be alright when he awoke the next day.

Except it wasn't alright, and Terence was convinced it would never be alright again.

Just as Max had explained to him, this Mrs Potts woman did come into the Fergusons' home every day, watering the plants in the morning and shovelling a handful of food into Terence's cage. Terence had tried to nuzzle against Mrs Potts's hand when she first approached him, but she had shrieked and swiftly slammed the cage lid shut.

Why would they ask this strange woman to feed Terence if she didn't like rats? It didn't make any sense.

So during that first week, Terence didn't receive any cuddles. He didn't receive any treats. And he most certainly didn't have the opportunity to run around and play.

Trapped in his tiny space, anxiety began to grow inside of Terence. With no concept of time – he was, after all, a rat, and didn't know his seconds from his minutes – he was convinced that he would never see his family again. He would be stuck inside his cage forever.

He had to get out.

But he knew it was impossible. He had scratched and nudged at his bars so many times before, but with no luck. What difference would it make now?

And so the second week began to crawl by, and Terence became more and more lonely. Every day he woke up to an empty house, briefly wandered around his cage alone, and then went back to bed. There was no point in staying awake longer than he needed to; there was nobody there for him. But sleep was becoming more difficult for the rat, as his mind started swimming with fears of eternal abandonment. He tried to convince himself that he was being irrational, that his family would return to him eventually, but it was no use. Terence was alone now, and he would be alone forever.

After thirteen days in isolation, Terence could stand it no longer. He was not the rat he used to be, gentle in nature and wishing for nothing more than an adventure. Now he had become frantic, panicking in a desperate attempt to escape the clutches of his prison. Overcome with a frenzied energy, he whizzed around his cage in the darkness, crashing into his food bowl and sending it flying across the other end with a clatter.

Terence paused to catch his breath as he panted. His head was throbbing. It felt like his heart was pounding inside his skull. He was sure he was sweating, his fur sticking with prickly heat against his skin.

He needed air. But what if he never found fresh air again? The rancid smell of an unclean cage filled his nostrils as he lunged onto the second tier. He picked up speed as he charged up and down, racing round and round, narrowly avoiding stepping on his own tail.

With a crash, he accidentally thundered into the cage door. He wobbled on his tiny feet as he fought for balance.

He regained his composure and turned to look at the place where his body had collided with the cage. It was then that he realised that the door had shifted a little. It hadn't opened, but it had definitely moved.

Wait a minute. What if...?

If Terence could summon up that same speed again, maybe he would be able to dislodge the door further. A few more pushes and the cage would be open. He would be free at last.

Not only was there nothing to lose by giving it a shot, but it was also Terence's last chance at finding happiness in a world that no longer included his family. Or so he believed, at least.

Terence bashed and crashed and stormed into the cage door, distributing the collisions across every part of his body until he ached all over. At last, however, his plan worked. On the final charge into the bars, the cage door swung open with a reassuring prang.

Terence almost laughed in disbelief as he stared, slack jawed, at his gateway to freedom. He moved cautiously at first as he edged nearer towards the opening. He was really going to do this, wasn't he? He took one final glance around his cage, before staring ahead. He counted to three, then charged, leapt, and landed on the carpet with a thud.

The doorway through which his family had left just short of a fortnight ago was barely a few metres away. He worked his little legs into a scurry as he raced across the floor, and scuttled with a flattened body straight underneath the gap in the bottom. He wasn't going to hang around any longer than was necessary.

A sudden blast of icy air hit Terence in the face, flattening his whiskers against his cheeks as he emerged onto the porch. The Fergusons' home had always been so warm; he never could have anticipated the chilling outdoor weather.

He shivered and backed up slightly, considering only for a moment that he should return indoors. But then a thought occurred to him: he always seemed to work up some body heat whenever he was running around in his exercise ball. If he just kept moving, he wouldn't feel so cold.

With his new plan, Terence scampered down the steps, across the grass, and out of the garden gate. Without looking, he raced across the road, down the street, through the park, and across the other side of town. Before he knew it, he was miles away from home.

It was then, as Terence realised that he probably wouldn't be able to find his way back to the house should he wish to return at any point, that a heavy, fat raindrop landed right on the tip of his nose. He glanced up just in time to see several more wet globules cascade down onto his face.

The rain continued to fall sudden and fast, at first coating Terence's fur in a slippery wash before drenching right through to his skin. He had never experienced this strange phenomenon before, had never been so submerged in water. He couldn't deny his fear as he charged through the streets, dodging lampposts and bins and the occasional human foot. He had to get away from the water. He had to escape the cold.

A short while later, Terence skidded to a halt. He had no idea where he was as he stood in the middle of the pavement, alone and dripping wet as the rain continued to fall. He did know, however, that he was too exhausted to take another step. He was truly defeated. With his bones bashed and weary, he curled up on the pavement and lay there, motionless, as a puddle formed around him.

Terence squeezed his eyes tightly shut as he fought to block out thoughts of his warm cage. His body shook against the cold wind and wet rain as he tried to summon up his own heat. It was no use. He continued to quiver and sniffle and whimper.

He had been so alone. Had tried everything to find his happiness. And now he was entirely on his own in the world. He had escaped the clutches of his cage, but the wider world had not been what Terence had expected. It was cold and wet and just as lonely. It was like one colossal cage of its own. All those thoughts of freedom, of a better life. What had he been thinking?

It wasn't that Terence hadn't appreciated his family. It was just that they offered only a small respite from his entrapment. It hadn't been enough. It never would have been enough. Their abandonment had given him the perfect opportunity to finally venture out to seek a better quality of living.

But now all he longed for was a warm hug from his family. The Fergusons were not there to comfort him though. Behind his eyelids, Terence could see the sky above him suddenly light up, which was quickly followed by a deafening rumble. The storm was brewing. He had to find shelter.

Forcing himself upright, Terence managed to crawl along the pavement, dragging his soggy fur across the dirty ground. Several steps later, however, and his mind told him that it was impossible for him to go any further. His tired body and his exhausted emotions were working in tandem to convince him that enough was enough. He had tried and failed. He had to give up now. His time had come.

Together, they encouraged his beating heart to pulsate more wildly as he struggled to calm his racing thoughts. Everything he had hoped for had been a lie. Everything he once cherished was a thing of the past. Everything in his new future alone in the world was dark and bleak and unbearable.

As the panic grew, Terence found he could no longer walk at all. Another grumbling release of thunder above him was followed by the burst of a thick, heavy raincloud that sent down an even heavier rainstorm. It was almost as if it had been aiming directly for Terence.

He could no longer control his heart. He shook and quivered as his eyes flickered into darkness. He couldn't see. He couldn't breathe. His entire body convulsed. He had lost everything. He was a lost cause. There was nobody there to save him.

Terence continued to shake until his heart began beating so wildly that its outline could be seen pounding against his chest, leaving an imprint against his wet fur. He screamed a silent scream as he felt his soul forcing its way out of his body. It tried to escape through his tail, but it was much too large to slither down the narrow space. Terence clamped his jaw tightly as he felt it creep up his throat. His legs twitched as his soul tried to exit out of each tiny claw.

It was no use. There was only one way out.

With a final pulse, Terence felt his body fling itself high into the air, before heavily landing back down into a puddle with a splash. Everything was silent, everything was still. It was almost over.

Almost, but not quite.

Terence's heart was finally motionless and his mind finally silent. He accepted now that he had tried but failed to escape his anxiety. He had not been able to cope with his life trapped inside a cage. He could not cope with the freedom of the uncertain and unfathomable wider world. Everything was quiet as he closed his eyes for the final time, preparing for his soul to take flight.

And his soul took advantage of this opportunity to escape its furry wet casing. As the rat lay still and alone in the freezing puddle, his soul burst out of his body, ripping up the carcass in an explosion of fur and skin and innards. Blood splashed against the pavement, mixing with the rainwater into a murky red pool. As Terence's soul whizzed up towards the thundering sky, he was at peace at last. He watched as he soared, heard the faint sound of his bones below cracking apart, the sticky wet noise of his organs slapping onto the solid ground. And finally, the last part of him to escape the clutches of his earthly body: his tiny little heart, pulsing no more, burst out of the limp rat skin, landing on top of a pile of shattered bones.

As Terence ascended higher, he took a final glance at his shredded body down below. His entrails were splayed across the pavement, swimming in pools of blood and rain. It was a sorry sight, but also a happy one, for Terence would never again have to suffer his inability to cope with a suffocating existence. He would never again have to fight against his own mind. He had said goodbye to his own imprisonment. As he disappeared beyond the clouds and out of sight, he smiled to himself, believing, whether rightly or wrongly, that his pain had come to an end.

The Fasting Girl

'Roll up, roll up! See the amazing Rodolphus and his magic chest! Meet our ginormous elephants up close! Be dazzled by our tightrope walkers and laugh at our clowns until your stomach aches!'

The Ringmaster of the travelling circus was seated in the carriage at the front of the parade. Two tall, muscular horses with ribbons tied through their manes pulled the remarkable vehicle along while he shouted through his megaphone.

'And don't forget to tell your friends! Tell your neighbours! Tell your neighbours' friends! We're only here until the end of the month!' he added as the crowd lining the streets stared in fascination at the display of peculiar costumes and mesmerising performers that passed in front of them.

The acrobats sprang around closely behind the Ringmaster, followed in procession by the animals, with the clowns tumbling away at the back. Just in front of them was little Emilia Babington.

Although she was only eleven years old, Emilia's life had already been full of such turmoil that that no child should ever have to face. The first ten years of her existence were spent alone with her mother as they struggled through each day inside a tiny, suffocating, damp room that was part of a house shared by three other families. The landlady was a bitter old woman who did not care for the hygiene of her tenants, and did not bother to keep up the maintenance of the building. As long as she was receiving her rent on time – something which was often a struggle for the

Babingtons – she held no concern for the gaps in the windows or the leaks in the roof, leaving the families to fester in the squalor.

Yet, despite Emilia's lack of opportunities for any education, and rarely spending any time with her mother, who sold floral embroidered napkins at the market in the morning and sold herself around the pubs in the evening, Emilia always tried to keep her spirits up. She was still a child, after all, and found joy in the simplest of things: the twinkling stars in the night sky; the way the sun lit up the streets of London on a warm day; the soft fur of the neighbour's pussycat as she stroked her hand across its back.

What Emilia loved most of all though was the circus. She had visited only one before, but the colours and sights and sounds had left such a striking vision in her memory that she defaulted to it whenever she felt sad. She could still picture the contortionists with their elasticated bodies, the trapeze artists fearless of height. The clowns throwing water, the majestic horses and their elegant riders. It was a world away from her own life, and Emilia had been enchanted.

Two years had passed since Emilia's visit to the circus, but it had only been two *weeks* since her mother's death. She'd explained to Emilia that she had caught some nasty bug from one of her clients, and Emilia didn't press her for further information. She was too overcome with worry not just for her poorly mother but for her own welfare.

The only person who had ever loved her, the only person from whom she could seek any company, was gone. She was an orphan now, a street urchin with no home and no family. Faced with little other choice, she had fled her excuse for a home when the landlady had threatened to send her to the workhouse. "They work young orphan girls like you to the bone," she'd explained in one of her rants about rent. Of course, Emilia couldn't afford to pay the rent now. But there was no way she could suffer the workhouse either.

All she could do as she disappeared along the murky streets of London was remind herself that it was a blessing that she had been forced to abandon her room during the summer months; the nights were still relatively warm, which helped to prevent her from catching her death sleeping in a doorway or down an alley. When winter approached though, she knew it would be a different story.

Not long after her departure, on that date two weeks after her mother's death, Emilia was shuffling her way through the market, her hands reaching out to passing strangers in a desperate attempt to gain something, anything, to eat. It made her feel uncomfortable, but if she didn't help herself though, nobody would. She was alone and desperate and had nowhere to turn to.

That was, at least, until she passed through the market, carried on down the lane, and turned the corner by the park. Emilia's stomach had been heavy with sorrow for so long now that she was certain she would never smile again, but the display in front of her was enough to widen her eyes in a brief moment of delight.

The circus had returned to town. The big top was erected in the middle of the grass, all bright colours with faint sounds of cheers and laughter drifting out across the field. A small queue of people stood outside, tickets clutched in their hands as they waited to enter the tent for the show's first evening performance.

Had she had any money to give, she would have handed it over without a second thought in exchange for the chance to experience the thrills of the circus one more time. But she didn't have any money. All she had was herself.

She thought about that for a moment. She had always been a petite child. There was even less of her now. Dare she consider trying to sneak her way into the tent with the rest of the crowd? She would definitely be small enough to slither among the crowd of people without anybody noticing her. But then everybody else was well dressed, presentable. She looked down at her arms and her bare legs. Her flesh was coated in so many layers of dirt and filth that she could barely see her milky white skin underneath. If she *was* seen, they would know straight away that she hadn't paid her entry, and then they'd call the police. And they'd send her to the workhouse.

No, she had to remain in the shadows.

And that's exactly what she did. Sneaking through the trees that lined the area, she managed to make her way around to the back of the tent without anybody noticing. Everybody on the other side was too distracted by a man performing on stilts and handing out leaflets to pay attention to anything else.

She approached the rear entrance to the tent – a simple flap through which the Ringmaster and the performers could enter and exit without being seen by the crowds. Reaching out a hand, she touched the fabric lightly, feeling the colours come to life in her fingertips. She had lived inside her own head for so long now, she wondered for a moment if she was just imagining it. But it was real, and it was right there in front of her.

Emilia glanced around her to make sure nobody was looking, and then gingerly shifted the flap to one side. It was heavier for her frail body than she expected, but she managed to open it enough to slip herself inside.

It was pitch black. She stood in the stillness for a moment, the sound from where the audience sat in the middle of the tent for the debut matinee much louder now that she was inside. She just had to find out how to get to the seating area, and hope that she could hide in the shadows, or maybe beneath an empty seat. It had been so long since she had enjoyed the circus. She was so excited about this one that she almost forgot the hunger that had been growing in her stomach. It was the escape Emilia longed for, even if only for the short hour of its duration.

She began to shuffle her way along the space, her hands pressed against the back of the tent to guide her. She could just about make out a faint light at the end of this corridor. That must be where the performers wait, she thought to herself. Wouldn't it be wonderful to catch a glimpse of them while they waited for their turn to perform?

She continued for a few more inches, satisfied that she was heading in the right direction, when her body collided into something. She let out a soft squeak before throwing her hand up to her mouth to muffle the sound.

For a moment, she wondered what it was that she had walked into. Perhaps it was a box of costumes or a crate of magic tricks. It would be so lovely to see them up close. She stretched out a hand to feel for the goods, but instead of finding a box of circus apparel as she had expected, she found herself touching something much softer. Something quite narrow and thin.

A leg. She was touching a person's leg.

A gasp escaped her as she threw her head up to see who was standing in front of her. With her eyes adjusting to the darkness, she could just about make out the blurry shape of a man.

'Well now, what do we have here?' He spoke in English, but with an accent Emilia couldn't place. 'Just what do you think you're doing in my tent, little girl?'

Before Emilia could open her mouth to respond, the man grabbed hold of the sleeve of her dress and dragged her towards the light.

To begin with, Emilia didn't notice the other person in the room with them. She was too fixated on the man who had dragged her there as she gawped up at him, absorbing his tall, slender frame. His face was narrow, with a pointed nose and an angular chin jutting out. Just above his thin lips was an equally thin moustache that curled up at either side. His eyes were sharp and beady.

'What you got there, Master?' came a voice from the other side of the room. A squat man with a high-pitched voice, wearing too-tight brightly coloured clothing, shuffled his way towards them.

This must be the Ringmaster! Emilia's eyes widened as she realised who it was she was standing before.

'What's the matter, girl? Cat got your tongue?' The Ringmaster sniggered.

'Isn't she a sight!' The squat man joined in with the sneer, his puffy cheeks turning red. The Ringmaster cast him a stern look to silence him.

'Quiet, Bumble. Give the girl a chance to explain why exactly I found her trespassing in my tent. I bet she thought she could enjoy our marvellous displays for free!'

Bumble nodded enthusiastically.

'N-no...I didn't...I wasn't...'

'Oh, you're speaking nonsense, child!' the Ringmaster interjected. 'Frankly, I don't care what excuses you're going to come up with.' He dismissed her whimpers with a wave of his hand. 'The real question is: what am I going to do with you now that you're here?'

'I think we should send her to the Peelers! I think I saw a constable out there just before!' Bumble suggested with an enormous grin.

'Oh, please, sirs! Don't fetch for them! They'd only send me to the workhouse, and I—'

'Workhouse, ey? And why might they do that?'

Emilia looked up at the Ringmaster through watery eyes. 'I—I don't have any place to live, Mr Ringmaster, sir.'

The Ringmaster scrunched up his face in a moment of deep thought as an idea began to surface. 'Bumble, are you thinking what I'm thinking?'

'That we go and call for the constable?'

A sigh. 'No, you fool. Girl, what is your name?'

'Emilia, sir,' she muttered.

'Well, Emilia, do you have any special talents?'

'Talents?'

'Yes. Can you do any tricks? Are you flexible? Can you perform?'

'Well, I...No, sir, I don't think so. But I—' Her brow furrowed into a crease of curiosity as she started to realise what the Ringmaster was suggesting. 'You mean something I could perform in your circus?'

'*Is* that what you mean, Master?'

The Ringmaster chose not to answer Bumble directly. Instead, he pondered for a moment as he looked Emilia up and down. She was a scrawny little thing with wide eyes and a petite face. The audience would eat her up.

'That's it!'

'What's it, Master?'

'Little girl – Emilia – do you know what a fasting girl is?'

She nodded. 'I do, sir. I saw one when I visited the circus when I was a little girl. She was much older than me – though I expect I am about the same age now.'

'And what age is that?'

'Eleven, sir.'

'Rather short for eleven, aren't you?' Then the Ringmaster muttered under his breath: 'Yes, I think this would work perfectly.' This time, louder for Emilia to hear: 'I bet you haven't had much to eat lately, have you?'

'No, sir.'

'And you've become accustomed to not eating, haven't you?'

'I guess so, sir.'

'In fact, you've become so used to it, so *good* at it, in fact, that one might consider it as, say, a talent?' His voice was raised at the end of his question.

Emilia looked as puzzled as Bumble for a moment, until she understood. 'Oh! You mean you want me to be a fasting girl? In your circus?'

A wide grin formed on the Ringmaster's face. 'That is exactly what I am suggesting, child. After what you have done today, I think you owe me your talents, at the very least. Wouldn't you agree?'

'I-I guess so.'

'So while I *could* send for the constable, I'm sure you'd much rather join my circus and travel around as my star fasting girl. What do you say? Would you *like* to be my fasting girl?'

Emilia's mind was now flooded with thoughts of colour and magic and wonder. She looked directly at the Ringmaster, who was staring down at her from his great height, and replied without any hesitation: 'Oh, yes please! I would like that very much!'

And so it was that Emilia joined the circus. She couldn't believe her luck as she spent her first few days absorbing her surroundings and making conversation with the other performers. Her own job wasn't too difficult; all she had to do was sit in front of her audience looking sallow and gaunt while the Ringmaster waxed lyrical about the wonders of the fasting girl. It wasn't a challenge for her, since the weeks she had spent living on the streets had ruined her complexion and caused her bones to protrude through her skin at her elbows and stretch taut across her collarbone.

And the parade! After a successful opening night for the circus, the company took to the streets the day after Emilia had joined the circus, and marching with the rest of the company was a thrilling privilege for the young girl. Seeing all of those people line the streets and applaud and cheer as they paraded through London sent shivers through her body. Although she had grown weary by the end of the day, she couldn't hide the smile that had stretched across her face.

The thing she most loved though was that she now had a warm bed to sleep on. It was a little lumpy in places, and sharing the room with several of the other performers meant it was always quite noisy, with lots of snoring and fidgeting, but it was much more comforting than sleeping on the hard ground outside in a doorway in the blackness of the night.

Of course, Emilia still missed her mother terribly, and wished so very much that she was with her to experience the wonders of the circus. But then if her mother *was* still alive, Emilia wouldn't be part of the circus now, would she?

She pushed back that thought as she lay on her bed, the blanket tucked up to her chin. She shouldn't ever think such horrible things. Of course she didn't wish Mama dead. She longed for her to return. But, with her natural childish curiosities, she couldn't help delighting at the new excitement that had unexpectedly developed around her.

There was one problem though for which Emilia had not anticipated. Her hunger was so crippling that she soon found it impossible to sleep.

She had learned to overcome her fear of stealing food when she was living on the streets. It was not a pleasant task, but a small piece of fruit on the verge of rotting or a sweet pastry that had hardened around the edges from the back of a stall was enough to comfort both her stomach and her mind to coax her into sleep. It was not a good life, and unbeknown to her she would not have been able to sustain it for much longer, but now she was facing a new kind of suffering.

She had forfeited stealing scraps of food in exchange for the warmth of a circus bed. Had she been asked which she'd rather have had the previous month, she would have declared that exchanging one for the other seemed like a fair bargain. Now though, she was truly facing the perils of starvation. It was the plight of *fasting,* she reminded herself. She was a fasting girl now.

But Emilia was also a smart girl. Even in her youth she knew that a lot of the circus show was little more than trickery. Never did she actually believe that fasting girls truly survived on air alone. She certainly never expected that the Ringmaster believed this either. However, it turns out that he was a great supporter of the authenticity of his performers. Emilia was his fasting girl, and fast she would.

She managed to battle her way through two more sleepless nights, tossing and turning, sweating one minute and freezing cold the next, while her stomach growled and yearned for sustenance.

Her body was growing wearier with each difficult breath she exhaled, her energy depleting as she fought to push away the hunger and the growing anxiety that was forming deep within her. It was no use. If she wanted to live – and she was pretty certain she did – she was going to have to do something about this.

If living on the streets had taught Emilia one thing, it was how to master the art of stealth. If anybody could successfully sneak food from the kitchen where the Ringmaster and the rest of the performers received their food each day, it was Emilia.

It was now or never, Emilia thought, knowing all too well how literal her words might become.

'Where are you going?' Charlotte, the teenage contortionist, whispered in the darkness as she felt Emilia shift from the bed beside hers.

'Shh, I won't be long!' she replied in a hushed voice.

'Well you better not get yourself into any trouble!' Charlotte bothered herself to say before turning over under her covers and returning to sleep without giving Emilia a second thought.

Emilia managed to slip out of the room without anybody else noticing her. At least, none of the other female performers spotted her as she crept out of the doorway. However, she didn't notice the figure standing at the other end of the corridor, who had managed to hide the flame of the candlelight he carried with him quickly enough to observe Emilia out of sight. Bumble was a rotten sneak, and of that fact he was incredibly proud. Just wait until the Ringmaster found out what he'd just seen! Nobody was allowed out of their room at night. Nobody, that was, apart from Bumble, the

Ringmaster's assistant. He would rush to him immediately to deliver his findings, and the slithering grubby little girl would be out on her ear before morning.

Unaware of what she would soon be up against, Emilia managed to reach the kitchen a few moments later with a sense of triumph. She eased the door open just enough so that she could squeeze through the gap, and began feeling her way around in the darkness for the cupboards as she searched for anything edible.

Aha! Her hand collided with the door to the pantry. She could almost smell the day's leftover bread that would be served with milk in the morning to the lead performers. Her mouth salivated at the thought of the doughy crusts as she creaked open the door, ready to slip inside and grab whatever her hands could find.

'And just what do you think you're doing?'

Emilia froze. The question had come from behind her. There was no shouting, no bellowing. Just a simple question from the voice she recognised as belonging to the Ringmaster.

Her mind raced as she frantically tried to come up with an excuse, any viable reason for why she might possibly be excused from stealing from the kitchen in the middle of the night.

Nothing came to her.

'Turn around, child!' the Ringmaster ordered, Bumble sniggering by his side.

Emilia knew she had no choice but to do as she was told. She let go of the pantry door and slowly rotated until she was facing the Ringmaster. With his jagged face dimly illuminated by the flickering glow of the candle onto which he tightly held, he looked even more sinister than usual. Emilia struggled to not show her fear.

'Well! Explain yourself then!'

'I—I—'

'Hungry, were we?'

Emilia nodded.

'Thought we'd have a little snack in the middle of the night, did we?'

Again, she could do nothing but agree.

'She's a thieving little madam, Ringma—'

'Quiet, Bumble. I know exactly what she is.' He leaned closer to her. 'She's my fasting girl. Aren't you?'

Another silent nod.

'And what do fasting girls do?' Her teeth were chattering; she couldn't reply. The Ringmaster took a few slow, echoing steps towards her, before speaking slowly: 'I asked you a question. What do fasting girls do?'

'They—they fast, Mr Ringmaster, sir,' she stammered.

'Well done. Aren't you a clever little thing? Well, I guess we're just going to have to be very cautious now and make sure that that's exactly what you do. You are a very good fasting girl, child. I know you won't disappoint me again, will you?'

His eyes were wide and menacing as he leaned forward to coax a response out of her. '*Will you?*'

'N—no, sir.'

'That's exactly what I wanted to hear. Now, follow me. Quickly!'

'Where are we taking her, Ringmaster? Are we throwing her

outside?' Bumble asked excitedly.

'No, Bumble, we are not.'

She wasn't going to be sent away? Emilia wasn't sure what was going on as she rushed to keep up with the Ringmaster's strides, Bumble barely a few paces ahead of her as his short, thick legs tottered along, slowing down occasionally to glance back at Emilia.

The Ringmaster gave no further explanation, didn't utter another word, until they reached a room Emilia hadn't seen before. The Ringmaster flung the door open and stepped inside, beckoning her – and Bumble – to follow.

To begin with, it was too dark for her to see anything. It was only when the Ringmaster paced in front of an object by the far wall that Emilia finally recoiled in horror.

'Oh, Ringmaster! You really *are* a genius! That's a *brilliant* plan! I never would have thought—'

'Shut up, Bumble. Now, Emilia. Do you know what this is?'

Fear had rendered her mute. She couldn't respond. She couldn't look at the Ringmaster as he spoke to her. She couldn't take her eyes away from the cage.

Once home to what the Ringmaster convinced Emilia was a ferocious lion, the cage now sat empty and awaiting its next inhabitant.

'Oh, I wouldn't worry too much,' he explained with mock assurance, 'you won't be in there all the time. You'll be allowed out to perform.'

Without another word from the Ringmaster, he pushed Emilia into the cage and slammed the door shut. The collision of metal on metal echoed around the lonely room as the Ringmaster stormed off back to bed, Bumble sniggering his way out behind him, leaving Emilia alone in the darkness.

Numb with shock, Emila was at first unaware of the tears as they dripped out of her eyes and down her cheeks. She had not yet fully comprehended what had just happened: five minutes ago she was moments away from filling herself with the comforting satisfaction of luscious bread, and now she was locked in a cage in the middle of the night, with neither room to move nor warmth to comfort her into a sleep.

Then the tears started tumbling thick and fast. Emilia let out a long, loud sob. Could anybody hear her? Would anybody come for her? She was frightened and alone, and, above all, she was still so very hungry and the pain was unbearable.

In fact, as the hours crawled by and Emilia remained without the knowledge of the time or how long it would be until she would be let out, the agony grew to such an intensity that the cramped conditions inside the cage made little difference as she doubled over in agony. She clutched onto her stomach to will away the pulsing that had begun in her core, receiving only mild doses of respite every now and then as she steadied her breathing and controlled her sobs as best as she could manage.

True to his word, the Ringmaster did come and let Emilia out of the cage just before show time. As usual, she sat on the stool in front of the audience while the Ringmaster explained to his gawping crowd the wonders of the fasting girl. More than ever, there was no need for Emilia to pretend. Her appearance was frightening, with her skin sallow, her cheeks hollow, and her eyes sunken. She heard the ripples of *ooh*s and *aah*s just as she did every night, except now she could not appreciate the bright colours or delight in the magic of the other performers. Now all she could see was a dark, eternal depression.

Emilia's demeanour only worsened as the new routine developed: she would be let out of her cage for her performance, before being escorted back to the dark room where she would be locked away for another night.

The rest of that week's shows ran as usual, and there were only a few left before they packed up and travelled on to the next destination. Once upon a time, any thoughts of visiting new lands would have filled Emilia with a great sense of excitement. Now though, as she lay curled up at the bottom of her cage, using her scraggly hair as a pillow, there was no energy left within her to consider what the future had in store for her.

Deep down, Emilia knew there *was* no future for her. Not now, not ever.

Uncountable days for Emilia with neither food nor water had taken its toll on the young girl. She knew now that fasting girls were just a ruse; one could not possibly survive on air alone. Her muscles and bones ached whenever she moved. She was too weary to lift her head, and her temples pounded in rhythm to the ringing in her ears.

Her tongue felt like wood in her mouth as it desperately sought hydration, her dry throat eager for any kind of nourishment to pass its way. Her stomach growled and yelled at her, but still she could do nothing about it.

Despite her fear of what the Ringmaster might do to her next if he disapproved of her actions, she knew that she would have to ask for something, anything, to eat. A small cup of water. She would not be able to perform if she could not hold herself upright. He had to give her *something*.

But Emilia didn't know how long it would be until the Ringmaster came for her, and none of the other performers were allowed anywhere near this room or even down the corridor in which it could be found, so it would be impossible for her to ask anybody else for any help. Perhaps, if she curled up tightly enough into a ball and hugged herself for some warmth, she might be able to sleep for a short while until it was time to be let out of her cage again.

Drawing her bony knees to her chest with the last of her strength, and pulling the hem of her dress around her ankles, Emilia tucked herself inwards - an easy but painful task for one with such a small, fragile frame - and rested her forehead on her knees.

She was not a naughty girl, she had just been a lost orphan eager to be part of a new and exciting adventure that could save her from a filthy, lonely life on the streets. What Emilia could not have known, however, was that, had she not joined the circus, her mother would have, in time, protected her from the heavens and guided her to a safe, secure new home. Instead, Emilia had been sucked in by the lies and deceit of performance, falling under the power of a ringmaster who ensured that his art was nothing but authentic, no matter what the cost. Now her mother's spirit could not penetrate the Ringmaster's blackened mind. Against her expectations, Emilia had become a true fasting girl, had delighted audiences that had travelled from all over London. Was that enough? Had that been her destiny? Or was she destined for more in life?

She would never find out. As she allowed the tears to distract her from the shooting pain that flooded her entire body as it yearned for its life, Emilia closed her eyes for the final time, leaving behind her crippling agony and the flippant frills of the circus as she returned to the soothing warmth of her mother's arms.

Hide Not Skeleton Love

Steven Skeleton loved Suzie Skeleton.

He tried to hide it, but the problem with not having any skin was that a beating heart was hard to conceal.

Whenever he jangled by Suzie, Steven's crimson heart would pulse wildly against the white of his ribcage. He could feel it squeezing in his chest as it threatened to burst out of his body and splatter at her feet in a mess of unrequited love.

At least, Steven assumed it was unrequited love. However, he had no real reason to believe this. Yes, Suzie had not shown him any love, but neither had he displayed his own feelings around her.

Whenever they passed each other in the park, as they so often did on their way to and from work each day, she would smile sweetly at him, displaying a set of perfectly formed teeth inside her jaws. They would occasionally exchange words, and the delicate sound of her soothing voice would always encourage Steven's heart to beat even more uncontrollably. However, he always held his bony fingers in front of his chest to conceal from Suzie the truth about how she affected him.

It never occurred to Steven than, while he had no idea how Suzie felt about him, the fact that he covered up his beating heart whenever she was around meant that Suzie too was unable to tell how he felt about *her*.

And if she did not know that she was the very reason that Steven was faced with constant heartburn and bruised ribs, it was always going to be an act of unrequited love.

All Steven needed was the confidence to show his heart to Suzie. If only she could see how wildly it beat for her, then maybe she would realise how he felt, and she too would reveal her own love for him. Knowing he had nothing to lose, Steven convinced himself that telling Suzie the truth would be worth the risk. After all, what was the worst that could happen?

So the next day after work, as Steven was sauntering through the park, he decided that today would be the day that he would finally reveal his true heart to Suzie. And right on schedule, she was heading straight in his direction as she approached him from further down the path.

He breathed deeply to calm his nerves – for even those with neither lungs nor a nervous system could suffer from anxiousness – and held his head up high. He looked straight at her.

'Evening, Steven!' Suzie said with a wide smile. Her eyes were large and round, and, had she any eyelashes, they would have fluttered in Steven's direction.

'Suzie. How are you?' he stammered.

'I'm great, Steven. And you?'

'Y—yes. I'm fine.'

'Are you sure you're alright? You don't seem well,' Suzie queried. 'Here, why don't we sit down?' She gestured to the wooden park bench that was conveniently situated beside them.

'Okay,' Steven managed, and they both sat their bare pelvises down. Suzie leaned back and rested her spine on the back of the chair.

Steven couldn't help noticing how beautiful she looked today.

He was sure she had had a polish, her bones looking smoother and more vibrant than usual.

His heart leapt about against his wishes. He flung his hand to his chest.

'Oh, Steven! What is it?!'

'Suzie, I—I have to tell you something. I mean, I *want* to tell you something.'

'What is it?'

She held out a hand and wrapped her fingers around his bony wrist, concerned for his health. She had ever seen Steven behave this way before.

Love could make skeletons do crazy things, but love could also prevent skeletons from doing things they desperately longed to do. This included stopping Steven from being able to find the right words.

'Suzie, I—I'm—I'm in—'

'You're in what? Steven?'

Despite a lack of glands, Steven found that he was sweating. He felt a fever rise to his head, and his bones began to shake from his skull down to his toes as he quivered with fear. He didn't know why he thought he could do this. He couldn't tell her, could he? What if she didn't feel the same way? What if she never talked to him again? What if she decided that it would be best to never see him again thus talking a different route to and from work to avoid him?

What if he was denied the very scent and sight of his true love?

It was too much. Steven's heart thrashed about uncontrollably. It crashed against his ribs, forcing Steven to clasp both of his hands over his chest to hide his emotions.

'I—I—'

It was too late. His heart had been strained too much. It slapped one final time against Steven's ribcage before slumping into an unnatural stillness. Steven's body crumpled onto the floor in a jumbled heap of arms and thighs and hips and fingers.

'Oh, Steven!' Suzie cried out as she rushed to scoop up his fragments. Suzie had never seen anybody's heart stop so suddenly before. She was shocked into a sudden grief.

The inquest suggested that Steven Skeleton had died from heart failure caused by stress. Nobody could have guessed, including Suzie Skeleton, whom he believed to be his skeletonmate, that he had died of a broken heart.

If Steven had managed to find the courage sooner, his life may have been spared. Perhaps he would have found out that Suzie felt the same way about him as he did about her. Love was difficult and love was painful, but Steven had not realised in time that the most dangerous kind of love was the love that remained unspoken.

Young

He held the silver frame tightly in between his hands as he stared blankly down at the photograph in front of him. Patrick had seen it a thousand times before, as it usually hung in the hallway at the bottom of the stairs. It had been their favourite photograph from their wedding day – their first mutual agreement as a married couple – and both he and Caroline looked overjoyed to be newlyweds as they flashed their smiles at the camera.

A few years after their happy day, however, Caroline's smile began to fade. Over time, it was as if she had forgotten how to smile at all. Everybody – their friends, their family, Patrick's therapist – assured him that nobody thought what had happened had been Caroline's fault. Not really. Nobody blamed her, and certainly nobody blamed *him*. But even now, as he sat there on the one-year anniversary of her death, Patrick knew he would always feel responsible.

Both of them had always wanted children, and they had planned to start a family as soon as they were married, but for Caroline it was more than a simple wish: she believed she was born to be a mother. It was her destiny to raise children and care for her brood. She had always longed for a large family too: maybe a boy and two girls, or perhaps two of each. At the end of the day though, she needed to have children. She would never be able to feel complete without them.

Unfortunately, Caroline never quite managed to have either a boy or a girl. There had been one occasion when she thought she had finally conceived, but she had been deceived by her own body.

She went to the doctor for tests. Patrick went to the doctor for tests. Both came back okay. There was no reason that neither the doctor nor the specialist from whom they sought a second opinion could see anything that would prevent them from being able to have children.

Caroline was beside herself. Patrick had tried to suggest the possibility of adoption, but for Caroline it was out of the question. She needed to feel her child growing inside of her. She needed to bond with her babies before they had even entered the world. She needed to be there from day one, from before day one, and there was no other way for her.

At her doctor's advice, Caroline started taking antidepressants. It was just supposed to take the edge off her worried mind – she was still young and still had time ahead of her to start a family – but after the first three days of her prescription, Caroline threw the pills down the sink, without her husband's knowledge. She was convinced that the medication would further harm her chances of conceiving. And what if she did become pregnant and then the medication damaged the child's development or, worse, caused her to miscarry? No, the pills were out of the question.

Perhaps, if she had continued to take them as everybody believed she was doing, she might still be here today.

As the weeks that followed turned into months, Caroline's mind began to deteriorate. As her mood depleted, the imbalance in her brain increased, and whenever the imbalance in her brain increased, her mood would deplete more rapidly. She was stuck in a treacherous cycle with no sign of any baby and no way out.

Caroline had started to take long walks, both to ease her emotional struggles and because she believed that the gentle exercise would make her body healthier and therefore more willing to give her eggs that could be fertilised. Sometimes she would walk through the park or down by the river, but sometimes she would saunter through the local village for a change of scenery. It was such a route that she had taken on that awful day.

The village was its usual quiet on the Sunday morning. There were a few people out and about doing a little shopping or enjoying a relaxing café breakfast, but Caroline was thankful that she didn't have too many distractions. Perhaps she would have benefitted from a busier morning, however, as at least then she might not have seen the pushchair.

By this stage, Caroline was prepared to do anything she could to have a child, and she was beginning to accept that perhaps it was simply biologically not possible for her and Patrick to produce a child together, knowing that she would have to consider other avenues soon. Maybe they could find a surrogate. She would look into it. She just knew that she needed to nurture and care for a child if she wanted her life to have any meaning.

This was exactly the thought that was running through her head on that morning when she locked eyes with the pushchair. It was a beautiful Edwardian carriage with large spindly legs attached to thick wheels, with a frilly white hood sheltering the baby from the sun. Caroline could not help herself as she approached to admire the infant.

She was surprised to see that the child inside the pushchair was not several months old as she had expected, but a tiny newborn baby, with reddened cheeks and head of black hair.

'She's lovely,' Caroline whispered as she gazed down at the little girl. She was dressed in a tiny babygrow that wasn't quite small enough for her.

'Thank you,' the baby's mother replied as she adjusted the hood on the pushchair.

'What's she called?'

'Emily.'

'Emily,' Caroline echoed. She felt the name roll across her tongue. It was beautiful. *She* was beautiful. In fact, as she admired her button nose and curious beady eyes, Caroline told herself that she really was the most perfect little girl.

It was the baby she had been desperate to hold for too many years.

'Oh, Harvey, put that down!' The baby's mother turned around for a brief moment to pay attention to her eldest child. As the woman wiped muck from the toddler's hands, Caroline's eyes flitted back and forth from the baby to the mother, and back to the baby, where they rested.

This was her chance. If she was going to do this, she had to do this now.

And she was definitely going to do this.

Without thinking about anything other than ridding herself of her permanent agony and finally being able to care for the child she had always longed for, she reached into the pushchair and lifted out

Emily. From the moment she touched her she knew that she loved her. She had never believed she could love another woman's child, but it turned out all she needed was to find the right baby to love. Emily was everything.

'What are you doing with my baby?!' Caroline heard the woman cry as she turned back around. Caroline couldn't answer though; the words didn't make any sense to her. It wasn't her baby. Emily belonged to Caroline.

She had to get Emily away from the danger as quickly as possible before this evil woman tried to snatch her away from her. They were a family now, Caroline and Emily and Patrick, and they would be safe together.

Without giving the woman a second glance, Caroline placed a hand at the back of Emily's soft head and stepped out into the road. She would be able to catch a taxi from the rank on the other side and take her daughter straight home.

So fixated was Caroline on saving her new baby, however, that she didn't see the van that was hurtling towards her. It struck her from the side, sending both Caroline and Emily sprawling across the road and into the oncoming traffic in the other direction.

It was instant death for the newborn baby, who had landed in the cradle of Caroline's arm as she hugged Emily tightly to her. Caroline had managed to curl up like a foetus as she wrapped her body around Emily, blood pooling out of the gash in her own head, before she too took her final breath.

*

Patrick wiped away the tears from his eyes and returned the frame to its hook in the hallway. Caroline had had a good heart. A kind, caring heart that had only wanted its own little human to love and cherish. If he had been able to provide her with children, she would still be with him, surrounded by their own adoring family. If he had suspected for even one second that Caroline had not been taking her medication then he would have intervened. He would have sought further medical help for her.

But he hadn't noticed. He had failed her as a husband and as her lover. It was not fair that she had died while he lived on. And that baby too. He had not been shielded from the sight of the tiny corpse when he arrived at the scene of the incident shortly after receiving a phone call from a witness who had known Caroline.

His own apparent impotence had cost the life of the woman he loved and that of an innocent, helpless child. He had ruined the life of that child's mother too, no doubt; he expected that losing a child would be more painful than never having a child at all.

It wasn't fair. It was selfish of him to have lived the past year of his life knowing that his own failures had caused so much damage.

He returned from the hallway into the kitchen and lifted out a knife from the drawer. He would take his own punishment. Maybe he would see Caroline again.

He held onto that thought as he gripped onto the underside of the table. Not allowing himself to overthink the situation any longer, he lifted up the knife and slashed it down repeatedly onto his wrist, accepting that, while life may start out full of hope and possibilities, not every family was destined to experience their *happy ever after.*

Business as Usual

There was something inexplicably magical about the way the glass-fronted high rises glistened in the sunlight. Like giant mirrors, they reflected the city around them, drawing in eyes and captivating London's residents and tourists alike.

Bill had always felt that way about them. From the moment he first walked into the corporate building on the morning of his interview twenty-three years ago when he was still fresh faced and eager to learn, he knew he had entered paradise. He took the elevator up to the forty-ninth floor that morning, delighting in its whirring as it rocketed him up to the penultimate level where he could enjoy the spectacular views from the shared office space. It was to be the beginning of the rest of his life.

Most days for Bill were similar. He would emerge into the office and dump his briefcase down onto his desk, before reaching for the cafetiere for his first caffeine hit of the morning. Then he would check his emails, respond to urgent enquiries, and finally observe his daily appointments. Board meetings would be followed by briefings, and then some data input at his desk before a quick working lunch. Indigestion would surface, and Bill would take a brief walk down the stairs to work off his food, before joining more meetings and conducting further telephone calls. It was all fairly routine, and very little took him by surprise any more.

To some, it would seem like a dull and monotonous existence. For Bill, however, it was exactly the way he liked it. He hated uncertainties. So when his superior called him into his private office one morning, Bill was a little taken aback.

'Bill, you know I've always admired you, don't you?' Mr Cliff – or Old Man Cliffers behind his back – said as he heaved his body into his leather desk chair, gesturing for Bill to sit in the seat opposite him. A combination of thirty long years at the top of his game and a few too many cream cheese bagels had rendered his movements slow and tiresome.

'Yes, sir, and I appreciate that—'

'I need you to do something for me, Bill,' Mr Cliff continued, not bothering to prolong the suspense, 'but I don't think you're going to like it.'

'O...kay? Am I allowed to ask what it is, sir?'

Mr Cliff leaned forward, his hands clasped together as he rested his weight on the surface of his desk. He released a sigh.

'It pains me to say this, but the company's not doing too good at the moment. We're simply not able to reach the same clientele that we used to. Competition is fierce now. We're swimming way, way out of our depth. You know what I'm saying here, Bill?'

'Yes, sir. I think so.' Oh, Bill understood, alright. Except he had no idea where this conversation was going. All he knew was that he absolutely could not afford to lose his job. He would be financially strained, but, worse than that, there would no longer be any meaning to his life.

'Here's the thing. I'm going to have to let some people go. I want you to decide who we can afford to lose.'

'Sir, I—wait, what? You want *me* to decide? You mean I'm not losing my job?'

A sudden spluttering cough overcame Mr Cliff. He covered his mouth with his fist as his cheeks reddened through the unexpected wheeze.

'Of course you're not losing your job! You're great at what you do. You know that!'

'Will all due respect, sir, so is everybody else who works here.'

'Yes. Well. As true as that may be, we simply cannot afford to keep running things the way that we are at the moment.'

'Perhaps we could relocate to a cheaper office?'

'I've already thought about that. It wouldn't make enough of a difference, and we'd still have to downsize to fit everybody into a smaller space. I'm not just talking about letting one person go, Bill. We need to reshuffle the entire structure of the company here. I completely trust you with this. Now don't worry, I'm not just throwing you in the deep end without some sort of buoyancy aid. I've prepared a list of names for you to consider. You can find it with Muriel at reception. She's staying, mind. Muriel and I have our own, shall we say, special agreement? But the list of names she'll give you, I need you to give it some serious consideration. Weigh up all of the options.'

'But sir, why me?'

'Because I know you'll make the right decisions. You've been here longer than anybody else, almost as long as I have in fact. You know everybody else inside and out. Now, if you don't mind, I'll let you see yourself out. I need to call my wife before she flips out again.'

With a wave of a hand, Bill was dismissed. He trudged off in the direction of Muriel's desk. Why him? Why now? Old Man Cliffers was right – he *did* know all of the employees inside and out. He knew their likes. Their dislikes. He knew who drove to work, who came by train or on foot. He also knew who had just taken out a mortgage on their new family home. He knew whose wife had just given birth to twin boys. He knew whose mother had suddenly taken unwell and had to receive private, expensive medical care.

And now he was going to have to decide which of those people were going to have their very quality of living ripped from right beneath their feet.

And it was going to be impossible.

For the next three days, Bill sat at his desk, profusely tapping the end of his pen against the edge of the wood, trying to come up with a solution. He hadn't slept. He'd hardly eaten anything all week. His energy was running thin, and he had only two days left to decide who was going to be told to pack up their desks and leave the company.

Of course, Bill was relieved his job was safe, but he almost wished that he could give up his position to save the others. It wasn't so much that he was a fantastically selfless human being, but rather that he was struggling with the pressure of the situation so much that any way out was an attractive option. Besides, he didn't have a family to feed. He was all alone when he returned home in the evenings, which allowed him more time to squeeze in a few more hours of work. It had helped him progress through the company. It had always been a desirable lifestyle for Bill. But now he wished he was at the bottom of the food chain.

What if he simply didn't pick anybody? What would happen if he didn't make a decision by his four o'clock deadline on Friday?

He distracted his thoughts with that idea for a moment, but could come to only one conclusion: it was probable – no, certain – that Mr Cliff would pick people at random to cast aside like used tissue, and it would be more than likely that he'd send home the wrong people.

Not that there was a *right* person. Even Jim in admin, who was frequently late and a little too relaxed, had his benefits. Everybody was an asset to the team in their own way. Internally, they functioned together expertly. It was the external factors affecting the company that was about to let too many people down

However, Bill tried to mask his growing angst. If any of his colleagues happened to glance over at his desk during the next two days, they never would have guessed anything was up. Whenever anybody approached him, he responded with a smile on his face. There was no need, he thought, to make anybody worried. Not yet.

As hard as Bill fought to come up with an alternative solution, however, Friday morning arrived and he could still see no way out. He was going to have to face the music and come up with a list of names for Mr Cliff, and he had a few measly hours in which to do it.

Lunch time was approaching and Bill was scratching his head while trying to concentrate on spreadsheets and infographics when he noticed Mr Cliff cross over the room towards him.

'All set for our meeting this afternoon, Bill?'

'Yes, sir,' he lied.

'Good. Look, I know it hasn't been an easy task for you, but you'll be rightfully rewarded. I promise.'

Oh great, that's exactly what Bill needed: praise for ruining the lives of others.

Bill didn't eat his lunch. He didn't finish his data chart or begin the presentation for next week's board meeting. He did, however, circle the names of those he thought would be the easiest to let go of.

And by easiest, he meant the least impossible.

With only half an hour until Mr Cliff called everybody into a surprise meeting for Bill to announce the news, he excused himself from the office and headed up to the top floor and out into the open air. A section of the rooftop had been designed to accommodate the needs of smokers and of those desperate for the respite of fresh air after an afternoon in a hot, stuffy office.

The rooftop was deserted on that Friday afternoon, save for Bill as he paced back and forth, his hands clasped behind his back one minute and nervously running through his hair the next. His palms were sweating. His knees were shaking. This shouldn't be his responsibility. There was so much pressure on him. How did Mr Cliff ever expect him to be able to deliver?

This was business, wasn't it? Being part of the corporate world could often be a beautiful thing. It came with many privileges, and, for Bill at least, brought a great sense of personal satisfaction. But the reality of it was: business was brutal. Everything could seem fine one minute, and suffocating the next. It wasn't fair. It wasn't right.

It was nobody's fault though. Bill knew nobody could be blamed. It's the way it went: one could go from financial security to being crippled by debt in the blink of an eye. It was not always foreseen, and rarely was there anything anybody could do about it.

This was his last chance, the final countdown for him to find a way out. He couldn't deliver the news to those six employees who were going to be cast aside. Eliza was the newest member – on paper, at least, it made sense to let her go. But she was a young independent with nobody to support her; she needed the security of this job. And then there was Arnold. He received one of the highest salaries; from the company's perspective, it would be logical to make him redundant to save a large pot of cash. But his family was expanding, and he needed to provide for his children. For every reason Bill could find to convince himself that he had chosen the right people, a much stronger argument in their defence came back to bite him.

He glanced at his watch. Ten minutes to go until he ruined life for six people. And their families too.

His pacing increased in speed as the thick leather soles of his shiny shoes hopped about on the flat rooftop balcony. He glanced out at the clouds above him as they stretched out across London. The city looked so vast and sublime from up here, with the sun low and shimmering across the buildings and over the river.

A bird swooped in front of the sun and soared across the sky. How free it must feel to float across this magical city. He wouldn't have to make any impossible decisions. Nobody would need him for anything.

Nobody would need him.

That's it.

Nobody needed Bill. He had never been bothered by that fact. He was too independent, a loner focused entirely on his career. It was a lifestyle that worked well for him. And now, with nobody to leave behind, no wife or girlfriend or children, it was going to work in his favour for him again today.

Bill had never been suicidal. He had had a pleasant life. But the recent pressure that had hit him with such an unexpected force had shocked the chemicals in his brain. Suddenly he no longer felt like himself. No longer thought like himself. A task was being asked of him that he simply could not deliver, and Bill in his current state of anxiety was unable to face up to that.

He had tried to convince himself that it was the way things were supposed to be, but as he took a few steps closer to the edge of the rooftop he knew that that was nonsense. Those words weren't going to provide any comfort to the families that would be facing homelessness because they could no longer make rent. It wouldn't support singletons in their times of need when their lack of sole income was unable to put food on their table or clothes on their back. It wouldn't bring anybody any hope when they were cast aside with barely a second thought.

Bill's heart rate increased as he placed his hands on the railings that ran along the edge of the rooftop. He had no idea whether they had been put up there to prevent accidental falls or if there was in fact a predicted high rate of attempted suicide, but he supposed it didn't really matter. Actually, he thought has he clambered over the railing and perched on the ledge at the other side, nothing really mattered any more. All he knew was that he would not be the cause of so much loss and misery.

He could not be the bearer of bad news.

Bill, who was used to working swiftly to tight deadlines, knew Mr Cliff would come looking for him soon. He knew he had mere minutes before he would be forced to deliver his verdict. In business, time was money, and it had to be utilised effectively.

And so, in his final few seconds as his entire corporate journey raced through his mind, Bill's body rushed down the side of the building with the wind billowing around the sleeves of his suit jacket, his tie flailing around his neck and tickling him in the face.

He was unconscious before his body smacked against the pavement below. He was dead before the hundreds of employees inside the building rushed down the stairs to his aid – or, perhaps more accurately, to gawk at the latest professional who had fallen victim to the suffocating demands of business.

Bill's death did not prevent half of Mr Cliff's employees being laid off. It did not save Mr Cliff any money by removing Bill's salary from the company's outgoings. In fact, it cost Mr Cliff a small packet as he was guilt-tripped into paying for Bill's burial the following weekend.

And the Monday morning after that, Mr Cliff and his halved workforce climbed into the elevator, whirred their way up to the forty-ninth floor, and sat down at their desks. Data was entered. Documents were filed. Presentations were finalised. Muriel greeted a host of potential recruits in the waiting room, each one eager to fill Bill's vital position and blissfully unaware that they were taking the job of a dead man.

Mr Cliff strolled into his office and took a seat in his oversized swivel chair. He had lost a dear, hard-working employee. It was a sad time. But Mr Cliff did not have time to waste being sad. After all, one can always rearrange the corporate ladder to benefit the company. He needed to use that time to build on his profits. He would never forget Bill, but everything had to continue as normal. Everything would still carry on without him. Everything would still be in operation, just business as usual.

Underwater

Parks are not designed to be dangerous.

On their own, without human interaction, they are not a threat. They are usually beautiful areas combining the splendour of nature with the joy of play. However, add in a human or two and they can, if mistreated, become hostile: foliage arson; stranger danger; pushing and shoving and fighting. Adults must always take care when spending time in their local park. For children, however, no amount of caution can eliminate the dangers of fun outdoors.

Mabel was not a very greedy child, nor was she one to worship a mountain of toys. She was very active, and loved running about in the fresh air or whizzing along the street on her bicycle. She had learned to ride her first bike with the assistance of her stabilisers when she was four years old, and, having had those stabilisers removed a few months before her fifth birthday, there was nothing she longed for more than a brand new, shiny bike.

Of course, Mabel's face was a picture of delight as she waltzed downstairs on the morning of her birthday to find her new set of wheels. The pink frame of her 'big girl bike' shone brightly, a strong contrast against the clean white wheels and matching handlebars. Pastel pink tassels hung from the rubber handles, the same gentle shade lining the spongy seat and the surface of her brand new helmet. It was the most beautiful bike Mabel had ever seen, and she longed to try it out.

Unfortunately, she had to wait for a few hours while her mother was at work, but as soon as she had been collected from her babysitter's house shortly after midday, she charged up the steps and through the front door of their home, and leapt straight onto her bike.

'It might need adjusted first!' her mother chuckled at her daughter's enthusiasm. But, much to Mabel's delight, the bike was a perfect fit.

Half an hour later, Mabel was cycling along the path in the park not too far from their home. It was a warm, sunny day, the beginning of summer creeping slowly in, but thankfully not too many people were around to obstruct her route as she rode her new bike round and round on the smooth path.

Her long blonde hair billowed behind her as she cycled against the breeze. The wind was cool against her dainty face as she worked up a slight sweat with her ferocious pedalling.

'Don't you want to rest for a moment?' Her mother was exhausted as she walked briskly to keep up with her daughter.

'Nope!'

'Okay, well I'm just going to stop here for a moment. I don't know where you get your energy from!'

'Can I keep riding?'

'Okay, but don't go too far away. Stay where I can see you!'

Apart from a few dog walkers and a couple of other children, the park was practically deserted; her mother knew Mabel would be safe enough.

While her mother rested on the park bench, Mabel raced along the path, pedalling at the bends and turning her handlebars with expert precision as she tested out her brakes on the shallow slopes. This new bike was perfect. She was going to take good care of it. The best care ever. She decided she would have to give it a name. Daddy had named his car, after all, and her new bike was even more magnificent than that.

'That's far enough!' she heard her mother call from the other end of the pond. Mabel had reached the end of the path, so she turned to head back along the other side of the pond. She would do several laps along the path that encircled the large stretch of water, but then she would probably need to retire to grab a juice. After all that cycling, she'd need a hard-earned rest.

'Be careful, Mabel!' her mother added as her daughter turned the handlebars to the right to take the corner around the pond. She watched Mabel rotate her head, her blonde fringe poking out of the front of her helmet, as she turned to acknowledge her mother.

She also watched as the front tyre of Mabel's new bike collided with the edge of the wall that ran around the pond, knocking Mabel off balance.

Her mother jumped up from the bench just in time to see Mabel tumble from her bicycle; with her head still facing her mother, she had been unable to steady the bike, sending herself slipping off the seat and falling sideways.

In the seconds that it took for her mother to race along the path to help her, Mabel tried to regain her balance, her arms flailing out in front of her as her feet became tangled in the wheels of the bike. With her helmet securely strapped to her head, however, she was weighted in a way that she was not used to, her head heavier than she was able to control.

Her mother was only halfway along the long stretch of the path when Mabel stumbled over the low wall and straight into the pond. Her bike fell onto its side, the back wheel spinning round and round.

Although the pond was not too deep, Mabel had not yet started her swimming lessons at school. As the water rushed through the holes in the top of her helmet, she waved her arms and kicked her legs as she sunk underwater. She was not a tall child, and, with her entire body submerged under the water, she remained out of sight.

The sound of her mother calling her name was distorted and distant as her body floated further towards the centre of the pond. Her helmet felt even heavier now as it remained suctioned to her head, forcing her further down to the bed of the pond. She fumbled at the strap with her remaining energy, but her hair had wound itself around her throat, rendering it impossible for her to grasp at the clasp of the helmet strap even if the murky pond water had not made it difficult.

As the pressure built in Mabel's lungs, her cheeks puffed upwards as if forcing their way into her eyes, threatening to burst her eyeballs straight out of their sockets. Her ears rang as her remaining energy escaped her slender body.

The last sound Mabel heard was the splash of another person jumping into the pond. She could not see her mother though as she swam towards her daughter; as the wheels of the bike on the path up above continued to spin feebly, a tardy siren faintly emerging in the distance, Mabel's eyes closed for the final time.

Robin Mutt: The Haunted Clown

For the most part, Robin Mutt was an ordinary kind of man.

He lived alone in an ordinary house in an ordinary part of London where not much happened and there was never a lot to look at.

When he was not working, he wore plain clothes, allowed his hair to sit naturally, and read the newspaper or took a walk in the park.

Yes, Robin Mutt was convinced that everything about his life was ordinary. Everything, that is, except his job. Whenever he mentioned what exactly it was he did for a living, conversations would often stop dead.

Take last week, for example.

Robin Mutt was waiting in a queue to post a letter – nothing special, just a cheque for a bill that needed to be paid by the end of the week. Dressed in beige corduroy trousers and a brown shirt, he was nothing striking to look at. However, an elderly woman behind him still acknowledged his existence – a rare occurrence not just for Robin Mutt but for any stranger passing through another's life – and started chatting. The conversation was nothing riveting, but enough to pass the time:

'This is taking forever. You'd think they'd have more staff on.'

'It'll be worse nearer Christmas too.'

'It seems to come around sooner every year.'

'It'll be snowing before we know it.'

'At least the weather is fine today though.'

'I hope it stays that way. I'm working outdoors this afternoon!'

'Oh, what do you do?'

'I'm a clown.'

And that was always the point at which suddenly nobody knew what to say to Robin Mutt.

You see, he used to tell people that he was a children's entertainer. But something about that phrase caused people to look at him funny – and not so much *clown* funny either, but rather *there's something wrong with you* funny. After a while, he became convinced that it made him sound like he shared a mind with criminals, so he started telling people that he was a clown. The looks weren't much warmer, but it was a start.

It hadn't exactly been Robin Mutt's childhood dream to become a clown. He had always been a very lonely boy though, and, without any real friends to keep him company, he used to write his own jokes to pass the time and provide himself with a little light amusement. It was just a form of escapism for Robin Mutt, a method of coping with his own fears as he locked himself away in his room during one of his parents' routine drunken arguments.

He didn't take any of it seriously though until he approached the end of secondary school. He had never bothered to read any of his creations to his parents in the early days, and with his father dead before he finished his education, and his mother estranged not too many years later, they never had the chance to experience their eldest son's humour.

However, one day, when Robin Mutt's younger brother was almost ten years old, he decided it was time to try out his material.

He read some of his latest question-and-answer jokes, and it was to Robin Mutt's delight that his brother found them hilarious.

It was that sound of his brother's hysterical laughter – albeit laughter for a joke that in hindsight probably wasn't that funny and was also too technical for the child to understand – that made him realise his calling. There was no sound quite like that of a merry child. It was warming, rewarding. There was no doubt in his mind after that moment: Robin Mutt was born to entertain.

Over the next few years, he learned a few other tricks that he could store up his sleeve: juggling, simple card illusions, balloon animals. He incorporated them into his act alongside the jokes, and the children loved it. Time and time again he would make the rabbit appear out of the hat, or stumble over air and land straight onto his bottom. Thank goodness for the layer of padding he'd sewn into his costume; it was just enough to withstand the bruising of his frequent tumbling.

Indeed, no routine was complete without his beloved costume. It was something in which he had always a lot of pride. Of course, in the early days of his career, when bookings were few and far between, and his income was sparse, he had worn something cheap and shop-bought, ill fitted and scratchy against his skin. As soon as he could adequately sustain the roof over his head and found that he had a little extra cash to spare, he decided it was time to invest in something a little more custom-made. A few weeks later, he was the proud wearer of a white one-piece clown suit and matching cone hat, both decorated with rows of brightly coloured pompoms and red lace frills that matched his short wig.

ROBIN MUTT: THE HAUNTED CLOWN

Every day before his appearance in front of his audience, he would stand in front of the mirror and paint on his elabourate facial features: a bright chalky white base, high eyebrows that were permanently surprised, large rosy cheeks, and a broad red smile stretching up to his cheekbones at either side. He would inhale deeply, smile with a genuine satisfaction and pride in his work, and add the finishing touch: his large, shiny red clown nose.

On this particular day, Robin Mutt carried out his routine as normal. He was performing at a birthday party for a seven-year-old boy and a dozen of his friends. Being the sort of gig Robin Mutt was used to, he was able to pull out all of his favourite moves: the balloon animals, the little flower on his lapel that squirted water, the somersaults in the garden that landed him straight onto his bottom in the middle of the moist grass.

As usual, the children roared with laughter, amused by the funny being before them, and grateful for their sugar-filled party bags handed out by the clown at the end of the performance. It had been a successful day, and Robin Mutt smiled to himself as he headed out the door and towards his car.

'Thanks for that. The kids loved it!' A hand slapped down onto his back as the voice spoke from behind him. Robin Mutt turned round to see the birthday boy's father in the doorway.

'You're welcome,' he replied.

'Honestly, I don't know how you do it. There's no way I could put up with that many children at once, and time after time too. You were great with them. You must have kids of your own?'

Robin Mutt suddenly found his heart feeling a little weighted.

'No,' was all he could reply. 'No, I'm afraid I don't.'

The conversation ended there, and Robin Mutt slipped into his car, changed into his driving shoes, and headed back home.

Home was the place where the heart was, so they said. But for Robin Mutt, home was the place where he lived alone. He had neither friends nor family to keep him company.

The truth was, Robin Mutt would have loved children of his own. But to have children, he had to find a partner first, a wife he could love and care for. But that was never going to happen, was it?

Slumping into the apartment block, he glanced only momentarily at the pile of post that had been left for him, before ignoring it and trudging up the stairs to the top floor. The steps creaked beneath the weight of his heavy clown shoes, the little squeaks in the heels of each boot giving off a little reminder of their presence with every step. It was a sound that usually made Robin Mutt bubble with joy, a reminder of how fortunate he was to have a job he loved.

But today Robin Mutt did not laugh. He didn't even crack a smile. Instead, he moped into his bedroom and landed without thought onto the edge of his bed. For so long, Robin Mutt had suppressed his loneliness, had managed to mask his deep-rooted desire for a family of his own. He never forgot how much he had adored having a younger brother. It was so uplifting to have somebody so youthful and full of an untainted love of life around.

After the fateful accident six years ago that took his only sibling's life, Robin Mutt vowed to himself that he would name his first-born after him. As the years ticked by, however, he forced himself to accept that it was an unlikely scenario. He grew increasingly convinced that he was destined to be alone until the end of time.

He pretended not to care.

But Robin Mutt did care. He cared very much.

For so long he had kept his emotions at bay. He didn't think about the family he didn't have. He forced himself to wash away the painful memories of his turbulent childhood. He couldn't face his own heart. He could make other people laugh, cheer them up, but he had never been very good at helping himself.

It turns out that the remark from the boy's father earlier that day was all it took for Robin Mutt to finally snap.

Enough was enough. As his mind erupted with decades of stifled heartache, his body became awash with numbness. He could both feel everything and somehow feel nothing at all. Everything he had kept hidden for so many years rushed at once to the surface of his emotions. They bubbled and boiled at the front of his mind. There was never going to be a change. He would never have his family. And he was never going to find that companionship he so ceaselessly craved.

He was going to be forever alone, and that was not a life he considered worth living.

With his mind racing into a frenzy, he pulled himself up off the bed and, half-absentmindedly, crossed over to the cupboard in the corner of the bedroom. His oversized clown shoes squeaked against the carpet. Tears trickled down his cheeks, smearing tracks into his white face paint. His actions were mechanical; he had given up, and his brain had become incapable of processing anything. If he was allowed to think about his actions, then that would lead to failure. And he couldn't fail at this. He had nothing left to give.

Nothing left to lose.

From inside the cupboard, Robin Mutt pulled out a large toolbox. It contained all kinds of hammers and spanners and screwdrivers that had barely been used. His eyes stared blankly in front of him as he took out each object in turn and placed them in a line on the floor. He worked slowly as he pulled out the remaining bulky items to finally reveal what he was looking for.

Resting beneath a pack of fresh sandpaper was a reel of thin blue rope. It had been purchased to hang up as a small washing line over the balcony of his flat, but he had never got round to it. Had he acknowledged that thought in the moment, he would have managed a slight smile at the fact that his own procrastination had, on this occasion, turned into a benefit for him.

And he did believe that it was a benefit. However, what he was unable to comprehend as he uncoiled the rope was that it was a benefit for nobody else. Nobody else would want this. The children he reduced to uncontrollable laughter, the parents whose lives he made easier by providing them with half an hour of respite during a manic birthday party, they wouldn't want this. They needed his skills, took pleasure in his talents, were thankful for his personality.

Robin Mutt straightened up on his knees and heaved himself upright. For a brief second, he stood there without moving, the rope dangling limp in his hands. But then something, a switch in the back of his mind, flicked and he whirred himself back into action.

His hands moved frantically and without control as he fumbled with the ends of the rope. He had no real idea what he was doing. Eventually, after several minutes of tugging and pulling, Robin Mutt had a knot with which he was content. Having been so focused on the task in hand, he had been too preoccupied to cry. His tears had dried up, leaving thick stains around his eyes and down his cheeks. He was void of all emotion now. The pain inside him was still there, still resting in the pit of his stomach as a dark, dense formation. But now, instead of encouraging him to crumble into a heap of broken thoughts and laments, it acted as his guide. It numbed him, commanded him, and he would listen to it. There was no other choice.

Living on the top floor apartment in an old building was a great convenience for Robin Mutt on this day. Where the lower rooms would offer flat ceilings, his attic bedroom presented itself with several rows of thick wooden beams. They had stood the test of time for many decades. They would surely withhold one man's weight.

Scrambling onto his bed, Robin Mutt managed to reach up and fix one end of the rope onto the beam. The frills on the cuffs of his clown suit risked being caught up in the knot, but he took care and managed to tie it without any damage. Somehow, that seemed important to him.

As Robin Mutt stood on the edge of his bed, his red clown shoes bright and garish beneath his white costume, there was nothing else left for him to do now. He picked up the other end of the rope that had been left dangling from the beam, and slipped it over his cone hat. It didn't occur to him to untie his hat from beneath his neck first; if he had been able to process any thoughts of his own in that moment and not those of his heavy pit of sorrow, he would have confessed to himself that removing his hat, complete with its brightly coloured pompoms, would have left him feeling incomplete.

Once the rope was around Robin Mutt's neck, he paused to inhale deeply. For a second, it seemed like his own thoughts were starting to take precedence. A few more minutes, and he may have regained control of his own mind. Just a little longer, and his actions would have been his own again.

But Robin Mutt in his present state did not want to waste any more time. As he exhaled, he lifted up his clown shoe and, after hovering it the air for only a fraction of a breath, brought the other one off the bed to join it.

It all happened in a matter of seconds, but for Robin Mutt it unfolded in slow motion. The ligature forced itself against his windpipe, tightening around his throat and cutting into his neck. With several inches between Robin Mutt and the soft carpeted floor beneath him, his body dangled in the air, supported only by the rope as he felt the pressure rise from his chest, through his throat, and up towards his face.

His cheeks began to puff out, burning hot and red as the pain that now overcame him raced towards his eyes. He could feel them bulging, his mouth swelling as he wriggled. It was a human reaction, an involuntary response. The rational part of his mind kicked in then, convincing him that this was not right. This was not how one should return to spirit. It would not answer his troubles.

He knew he had to free himself from the strain.

He was about to reach up a weak hand to prise the rope away from his neck, but it was too late. Time was up for Robin Mutt.

His body swayed back and forth as it hung from the beam, a remnant of his fight to save his own life. His hat had remained in place, only cocked slightly to one side as his head had leaned sideways.

It had been a snap decision, brought on by years of denying his true fears and suppressing his eternal loneliness. The slightest trigger had brought them rushing to the surface, and they had burst out of him like a storm of candy tumbling from a piñata.

And now, as his skin was mottled red and his neck lined with a deep bruise, he had become nothing but an empty shell. There was nothing left inside of him, nothing there at all. Robin Mutt would never smile again, and instead of the merry sounds of laughter that once presided, there would only ever be silence in its wake.

The Girl in the Well

Under normal circumstances, Poppy Anna was a well-mannered, respectful little girl.

She would tidy her bedroom when she was asked. She would never make a fuss about eating her vegetables. And she never, ever spoke back to her parents.

This was Poppy's nature, at least, until a few months after her eleventh birthday. Her mother had brought home a special treat for her to enjoy after dinner: Poppy could smell the rich chocolate sponge of the cupcake through its box, could almost taste its smooth buttercream icing as she inhaled the aroma with her nose pressed tightly to the edge of the box. She salivated at the thought of sinking her teeth into the dessert.

'Go on then, you can eat it now!' her mother declared with a smile, setting a glass of milk down beside the cupcake.

And so Poppy chewed and licked and swallowed until the cake was gone and her stomach was almost full. Then, with barely any room left, she scooped up the crumbs with a finger, and popped them into her mouth. She washed it all down with a large gulp of milk, before leaning back in her chair and wiping at her mouth with the back of her hand.

She turned to thank her mother, but noticed that she was staring straight at her. In fact, now that Poppy thought about it, her mother had been watching her a little too closely the entire time.

'Mum?' Poppy asked with a puzzled expression.

Mrs Anna's smile stretched from one ear to the other. 'Yes,

dear?' Her voice was sickly sweet. It was the voice she used whenever she was trying to hide something from her daughter.

'What's up, Mum?' Poppy raised her eyebrow to try and coax the information out of her.

'What?' her mother replied with a shrill tone. 'What makes you think anything's up?'

Poppy cast her eyes down at the empty plate in front of her and then looked back up at her mother. She burrowed the silence deep into her guilty face.

Eventually, her mother's expression collapsed into a heap of frowns and wrinkles. 'Oh, alright.' She paused, took a breath. 'I know how you feel about having one, but I've found you a nanny. She'll be here tomorrow to meet you before—'

'*What?!* The cupcake suddenly felt very heavy as it rested like a rock in the pit of Poppy's stomach. 'That's what the cake was for, wasn't it? It was a bribe! Oh, Mum!' she wailed. 'I told you I don't *need* a nanny! I'm old enough to take care of myself!'

Poppy slammed a hand down onto the table in protest, narrowly avoiding sending the plate crashing onto the floor.

'Look, I know you think you're old enough now to stay home on your own, and your father and I agree that you're a very sensible girl.' She reached to stroke Poppy's hair, but she flinched and shifted away from her in her seat. Mrs Anna sighed, before continuing: 'It's not you, Poppy. It's other people. With your father's new job, we're both going to be working really late, and you just can't stay in the house by yourself after dark. It's not safe.'

There was nothing but silence as she waited for Poppy to

reply.

She said nothing.

Instead, she slid herself out of her seat, folded her arms across her chest with an exaggerated groan, and stomped off to her bedroom to be alone, not uttering another word to her mother for the rest of the evening.

Unfortunately for Poppy, she was learning that, once grownups had made a decision, their word was final. And so it was that, at three o'clock promptly the following day, there was a confident knock at the front door. Poppy's new nanny had arrived.

Poppy hid at the top of the stairs out of sight as she peered around the corner to watch her mother open the door to let this stranger inside. What was revealed in the doorway was not at all what Poppy had expected. Her new nanny looked positively *normal.*

Miss Draconity, as she was later introduced, was a tall, slender woman of middle age, with dark hair tied in a bun at the nape of her neck. Two beady eyes were positioned above a narrow nose, while on her forehead sat two eyebrows that were almost permanently arched. With winter just around the corner, and the cold, bitter wind increasing, she was dressed in a long, black woollen coat with a black scarf wrapped around her neck. She removed this, and handed it to Mrs Anne as she invited her into her home.

'Thank you, that would be lovely,' Poppy heard Miss Draconity say as her mother offered her a cup of tea. To Poppy's surprise, her voice was quite delicate, not at all booming and threatening like she had anticipated.

'Come down and meet Miss Draconity, Poppy, dear,' her mother beckoned as she spotted Poppy at the top of the stairs.

Poppy skulked downstairs, pressing her weight into the banister as she slid against it, forcing herself to smile in front of her mother as she stopped in front of Miss Draconity. She curtseyed, just as her mother had instructed her to do when she had briefed her earlier that day.

'Oh, isn't she charming!' Miss Draconity declared with sincerity. Poppy's stomach lurched. There was no way this Miss Draconity – Miss *Dragonlady*, Poppy thought to herself as she tried to hide a giggle - was going to stick around for long. Poppy was old enough to look after herself, despite what her mother thought, and that was that.

Three nights a week, Miss Draconity picked up Poppy from school while her parents were at work. Poppy grumbled all the way home, dragging her feet behind her and scuffing the toes of her school shoes as she traipsed a few metres behind.

'Hurry up, madam, or there'll be no snack for you!' Miss Draconity declared on more than one occasion. She had spoken light-heartedly at first, but after a few consecutive nights of being forced to encourage Poppy to pick up the pace, it became obvious in her tone that she was becoming quite frustrated with the child's disobedience.

Still, she couldn't have known that Poppy loathed being called *madam*. It was so revolting! No way was she going to listen to the Dragonlady if she was going to call her such disgusting names. On one occasion, Poppy decided to inform her that she most certainly was *not* a madam, and that the Dragonlady had *no* right to speak to her like that.

Well, Miss Draconity didn't rise to Poppy's taunt immediately, but as soon as they were in the house and Poppy had raced to the biscuit barrel, her nanny knew that this was the perfect opportunity to discipline the child.

'You dare speak back to me like that again, *madam*, and I'll make sure you don't eat any snacks for the rest of the month!' She threatened her with her hand placed firmly over the barrel just as Poppy was about to reach in for a cookie. 'I've put up with this backchat and ignorance from you for long enough now. Things are going to change around here!'

The sudden outburst from the Dragonlady had taken Poppy so much by surprise that her mouth hung open, slack from shock as she struggled to respond. Had she even asked a question to which Poppy was expected to respond? She was stunned. She had never heard the Dragonlady raise her voice like that before. After two weeks of looking after Poppy several evenings a week, Miss Draconity had finally snapped.

From that moment, after Miss Draconity sent Poppy up to her bedroom with nothing to eat, she would never again address the child in the sweet-natured, considerate manner than she liked to use with the other children she looked after. Poppy was not her equal;

she had not earned her respect. She spoke to her calmly only when Mr and Mrs Anna were around. Otherwise, Poppy received the authoritative tone she deserved and nothing more.

However, despite Miss Draconity's intentions to discipline Poppy, boundaries began to be stretched even further: Poppy refused to brush her teeth at the Dragonlady's command; she wouldn't wash up the dishes after mealtimes; and when it was time for lights out, Poppy was still propped up in bed with her nose in a book.

And the more Poppy disobeyed the Dragonlady, the angrier the Dragonlady became.

The weeks went on, and Poppy was beginning to consider the idea that this pointless nanny would never leave. Every day she whined to her parents, tried her hardest to convince them that she absolutely did not need a nanny. Nothing she seemed to do or say was working though. If she wanted to see results and get rid of the Dragonlady once and for all, she was going to have to up her game. After all, no nanny could suffer a truly disobedient child for too long, could they? If the Dragonlady thought Poppy was an unruly child so far, she was in for a real shock.

And so, the next day after school, Poppy and Miss Draconity were sitting at the dining table for their evening meal when Poppy decided to take the opportunity to hatch the first stage of her plan. In two days' time, the final month of the year would arrive, which meant it was almost pitch black outside by the time she arrived home from school, and the ground was still slippery wet thanks to the non-stop rain from over the last few days. It was the perfect condition for her plan.

'Miss Draconity?' she said in her most polite, respectable voice, suppressing the urge to throw up in her mouth.

Miss Draconity paused, her fork midway towards her mouth, only for a moment. 'Yes?' She responded nonchalantly, before gracefully placing the piece of potato into her mouth and chewing delicately, trying to hide her surprise at Poppy's sudden display of manners.

'Could I go outside into the garden once I've finished eating, please?' Poppy gave her nanny the largest, friendliest smile she could muster. She was convinced she deserved an award for her acting abilities.

Miss Draconity fought to not show her increasing astonishment at this awful child's sudden politeness. It was, of course, far too dark to allow her to play in the garden at this hour, but she couldn't outright deny the child her wish – efforts should be rewarded, and if she wanted to teach Poppy that manners were effective then she would have to appear to consider her request.

She pursed her lips in thought, before replying: 'Okay, you may go outside, but only if you eat all of your vegetables.' It was a foolproof response, or so she thought. Poppy *never* ate the vegetables she cooked for her. There was no way she would be going outside tonight.

'Okay!' Poppy replied as she shovelled a ginormous pile of peas into her mouth. The look on the Dragonlady's face as her jaw hung loose in shock was only the beginning of Poppy's satisfaction.

*

Ever one to look upon liars in disgust, Miss Draconity forced herself to remain true to her own word. She made sure Poppy wrapped up warm, padding her out with several woolly layers, before bundling her out into the garden with the firm explanation that she had half an hour and not a second longer.

Well, thought Poppy, that was plenty of time to put her plan into action. First, however, she allowed herself to spend a short while genuinely having fun, rocking back and forth on the wooden swing and trampling her wellington boots though piles of golden brown leaves.

'Fifteen minutes!' Miss Draconity called through the open kitchen window once the halfway mark had arrived.

This was Poppy's chance. When the Dragonlady came out to collect her after she would refuse to come inside, she would take one look at Poppy and refuse to ever return to the house. There was no way she could remain in charge of such a naughty little girl. And even if she didn't leave, as soon as Poppy explained to her parents what the Dragonlady had allowed her to do, she would be dismissed immediately. She had to be.

Poppy skipped down to the bottom of the garden where the old well had been built. Her parents had covered it up with a thick, heavy slab of concrete when they first moved in so that it would be safer for Poppy to play in the garden without fear of her accidentally falling in. They always said they would have it properly filled in one day, but neither of them ever remembered to do anything about it. Now that Poppy was older, she was trusted to be careful around it and not clamber onto it, so there was really little rush to do anything about it. It turned out to be a blessing for Poppy.

She glanced back towards the house to make sure she wasn't being watched, before turning back to face the well. Bracing herself, she placed her palms against the side of the concrete, and pushed.

It didn't budge.

She was going to have to use all of her body weight if she wanted to shift it. She repositioned herself so that she could lean in with her torso, forcing herself into the concrete until it crept forward a little. Her eyes widened in delight as she felt it moving even more, the concrete slowly grating across the top of the well.

The ground beneath her was wet and slippery as she struggled to keep her balance, but eventually she managed to move the cover halfway across. With the concrete slab hanging off the edge now, she found that all she needed to do was apply a little pressure from the other end to tip it over.

It landed on the grass with a thud. Panicking, Poppy shot her eyes in the direction of the kitchen window. The Dragonlady was bound to have heard it. Besides, the clock was ticking now, and she would soon come outside to drag Poppy back inside, so she was going to have to act fast if she wanted her plan to work. And, in that moment, there was absolutely nothing she wanted more. There was no way she could stomach another evening with that vile, controlling woman.

Not wasting any time, Poppy pulled herself up onto the wall that ran around the well. It wasn't very thick, only one brick wide all the way around, but it was high enough that it came up to Poppy's

116

chest. She knew she would have to be careful not to fall in, but she was a sensible girl and didn't move too quickly for fear of losing her balance. She used the wooden beam across the top of the well's roof to steady herself as an extra safety measure. After all, this was just a prank. It wasn't meant to be too dangerous.

With caution, she managed to manoeuvre her body until her bottom was firmly planted on the wall, her legs dangling down as she gripped onto the beam. All she had to do now was wait.

And wait.

And wait.

The minutes felt like hours as Poppy kicked her heels against the wall. The wind was beginning to nip at the skin of her cheeks, and she longed for nothing more than one of Miss Draconity's hot, sweet cups of cocoa.

Not that she would ever admit to the Dragonlady just how delicious her cocoa was. But maybe she'd offer her some when she went back inside. Just as soon as she came out to collect her.

Eventually, Miss Draconity appeared in the dimly lit doorway, which she'd opened ajar just enough to stick her head out. But Poppy was too far away to be seen through the darkness. The Dragonlady would have no choice but to come out into the garden.

Oh, she was going to flip when she saw Poppy playing by the well. She just knew it. Any moment now.

'Poppy?' Miss Draconity called as she took a few steps forward, opening the door wider so that the light from the kitchen flooded out to make a path onto the patio. She shuffled in her slippers across the ground until her toes collided with the wet grass.

117

It was then that she noticed her.

'Poppy!' she shrieked, her hands rushing to her chest. 'What on earth are you doing, you silly girl?!'

Spurred by fear for the child's safety, Miss Draconity lunged forwards as if to pull her away from the well. Unfortunately, she missed her footing in the darkness, kicking a rock instead, and lost her balance as her flimsy footwear slipped away from her feet.

As Miss Draconity flew through the air, landing on the floor in a heap, Poppy threw her hand in front of her mouth to cover her gasp.

And that gasp – a single, barely audible display of Poppy's natural compassion for her nanny – was all it took. No longer gripping onto the wooden beam, Poppy's own balance became unstable, forcing her backwards as her youthful frame tumbled off the wall and down into the old well.

Down, down, down she fell, her scream echoing all the way to the bottom. Her landing sent a muffled thud and remnants of a splash back up to the top.

By then, Miss Draconity had scrambled to her feet. She sprang to peer down the well, but Poppy was in its deep base now, among the freezing water and jagged debris; there was no way she could be seen.

'Poppy?'

The only reply was the sound of Miss Draconity's own voice echoing back up at her.

Was it possible that Poppy had survived the fall? Was there any chance at all that she was simply too injured or too weak to respond? The well was deep, probably deeper than anybody would have guessed, but what if there was still time to fetch the child out? To rescue her?

Miss Draconity thought about this for a moment, but a sudden sharp pain around her knee from where she had fallen was enough to pull her away. What had Poppy been doing playing by the well anyway? And why wasn't it covered up? She was such a naughty, wicked child. No doubt she had been trying to wind her up as usual. Perhaps she didn't want to help the child out after all.

And even if she did call for help, what would happen to her job? She'd never work again if the parents thought she had anything to do with this. She lived alone, wouldn't be able to make rent without a job. She'd be homeless and living on the streets before she could blink. And it would all be because of one silly, selfish little brat.

Miss Draconity had made up her mind. It was out of the question that she should bother trying to see if the girl was still alive. She would be beyond help now, and it would only risk the lives of others if they had to send somebody else down there to fetch her. Firemen had much more important work to do, didn't they?

Driven partly by concern for her own welfare and partly by anger at this stupid girl's actions, Miss Draconity's mind ran on autopilot as she summoned all of her strength to lift the concrete slab back onto the well. Not a sound emerged from below while she worked. There was no way the child was still alive. It just wasn't possible.

With her grass-stained stockings and slightly guilty conscience, Miss Draconity took off into the night as she fled from the house without ever looking back. The dead child was not her problem.

Did Mr and Mrs Anne try to contact Miss Draconity once they arrived home later that evening to find both their daughter and her nanny missing? Of course they did. Then they phoned the police. Went out searching for the pair. If neither of them had turned up by morning, an appeal would be broadcast for Poppy. But since they couldn't provide any details of Miss Draconity's address, or even her full name – that was the problem with people who were too quick to trust others, particularly those who had been recommended only by a friend of a friend – they were told that there was little else they could do without being able to provide further information.

Of course, the Annes never saw Miss Draconity again, and Poppy didn't turn up the next day, or the day after that, or any other day for that matter. Over time, they learned to talk through their grief, accepting the loss of their daughter, and managing to pull their way through their lives. All that time, they remained completely unaware that their young daughter's corpse was lying at the bottom of the well in their own garden, slowly rotting away day by day, year by year, until her parents were both long gone and Poppy's skeleton was nothing more than a pile of old, forgotten bones.

Organs Suckled to Inorganic Demise

As far as the idyllic streets of suburbia were concerned, Nettle Row was a shining example of the peaceful quality of life that residents could enjoy. Nothing out of the ordinary ever occurred there. Day was day and night was night. Black was black and white was white. Everybody knew everybody else, and the neighbourhood was built on a foundation of trust and support. If Mr Jenkins at number six needed to trim his grass, somebody would be on his doorstep brandishing secateurs before he could reach for his gardening shoes. Whenever Mrs Oswald from number fourteen was faced with bare cupboards, several of the resident teenagers would rally together and fetch her shopping for her. Of course, she would offer them a shiny penny each for their trouble, but they always refused to accept it. After all, what were neighbours for if not for helping one another out?

Now, while it was true that all of the residents were pleasant and approachable, there was however one particular character who rarely made an appearance. She did not attend the annual July the Fourth street party. She did not help decorate the community's Christmas tree at the beginning of each December. When Arnold Potts's little dachshund went missing for almost an entire day, she was the only one who did not trek through the woods at the back of the estate to help find the lost puppy.

It wasn't that this resident, who was known to her neighbours only as Old Lady Jenkins from number twenty-three, was inhospitable. She was not rude, nor did she consider herself to be

121

too important to converse with the rest of the street. It was simply the case that Old Lady Jenkins was a social recluse. She left the house only to visit the corner shop, where she spoke briefly and politely to Mr Darwen the shopkeeper, handing him over his latest supply of jam she'd made fresh from the fruit grown in her garden in exchange for a small fee, before shuffling her way back home and bolting the door firmly behind her.

Perhaps Old Lady Jenkins had never had any friends before. Her relationship with Mr Darwen was purely business, and, despite the fact that he always made an effort to strike up a conversation with her about the weather or the latest stories in the newspapers, Old Lady Jenkins never engaged in small talk.

'I do not read the news,' she would mutter before bidding him goodbye.

The truth was, nobody knew why she spent her time alone. It was almost inconceivable to the other residents that she would *enjoy* such a hermit lifestyle, but it seemed to suit her well. She was a mystery that sent whispers through the houses whenever she was spotted. And if she had provided Mr Darwen with a new type of jam for his customers, the families of Nettle Row would all be eager to try it, debating where she got her recipes from.

'Do you think they're in a book from Barnes and Noble?' somebody would suggest.

'I hear it's an old spell book,' another person would utter.

'You think she's a witch?' asked somebody else.

'They say her family has lived on this street for years. They also say that, on the night that she was born in that very house, a bolt of lightning struck her back garden as if to welcome her into the world.'

Who *they* were was always unclear, but the rumours were always the same: Old Lady Jenkins had grown up on Nettle Row, was now suspected to be in her eighties, and was the longest remaining resident. She had seen so many people come and go over the years. She probably knew all of their secrets. For some, it was fortunate that she did not speak to her neighbours, or ugly truths spanning decades would risk being spilled.

Old Lady Jenkins was not unaware of the rumours that circulated. If she wanted to, she could comment on them. She could try to dispel them if she was bothered. But she was not concerned. Although she would never openly declare her powers, she would never deny the truth either. She was not ashamed of who she was.

Yes, it was true. Old Lady Jenkins was a witch.

She did not wear a black hat or a cloak, and she did not have a pointed nose. Her fingernails were clipped neatly, and her skin was free from warts. Her grey hair was long enough to cascade down to her waist, but she always kept it tied neatly in a bun at the back of her head. As far as traditional witches in fairy stories were considered, she was unconventional, practically unrecognisable as a witch. She would probably be a great disappointment to the fantasies of Nettle Row. However, there was one characteristic about her that, if anybody were to witness it, would instantly suggest that she practiced witchcraft.

Yes, Old Lady Jenkins was very fond of her cauldron.

In fact, she was so fond of it that there was always something bubbling away in the cast iron pot. It hung over the large aga in her kitchen, the flagstones beneath catching any stray embers while she brewed berries and plums and apricots ahead of filling her jam jars. She would then scrub it clean with an old wire brush, and unlock the pantry that was half hidden by an old wicker chair to reach for whatever potion bottles she required for her nightly ointment.

As a general rule, Old Lady Jenkins was a good witch. Her ointments reduced her wrinkles, eased the aches in her bones, and filled her home with delicate fragrances to soothe her to sleep. She stored the ingredients in little glass bottles of different colours, each one labelled with a hand-written note to display the name, shelf life, and strength of the liquid. Even in larger doses, however, they would all be fairly harmless to a mortal.

However, on the very top shelf in the pantry, Old Lady Jenkins stored a small selection of heavy glass decanters. They were filled with thick, syrupy black liquids, each one repugnant in smell and revolting in appearance. If one of these liquids were to be mixed with any of the potions on the lower shelves, it would reverse the intended effects. They were the spells of the dark witch, and Old Lady Jenkins had so seldom used them that the decanters had gathered a thick layer of dust around them, a collection of cobwebs stringing from the cork stoppers.

Every few decades, however, an occasion would arise for which Old Lady Jenkins knew the decanters would be essential. Two weeks after the Carmichael family moved into the home next door, she knew that such an occasion had arrived.

*

Michael Carmichael was a lively, energetic boy of nine years old, with a healthy appetite and a hearty love of the outdoors. It was a blessing to his parents that he spent his free time in the garden, breathing in the fresh air instead of choosing to remain indoors like many other children his age would do. In fact, the large garden of their new home, with its rows of neatly trimmed hedges and patterns of paving stones from which Michael could leap around, provided him with an essential sanctuary. He had been upset to leave his old home and his old friends behind, but he could channel all of his energy into exploring this new space.

They had the weather for it too that spring. The flowers were blooming nicely, and Michael took care in admiring their delicate petals as he absorbed their individual colours. Lilacs and navies and fuchsias flourished in patches around the fresh grass as Michael kicked his football or batted the tennis ball against the garden wall or swung on the tire swing that had been fixed to the branch of a tree.

Michael had always loved trees. He admired their stocky trunks and billowing branches. He loved to climb them and swing from them and drop back down to the ground with a triumphant thump. The trees in his new garden were particularly magnificent; he knew that, once fall had arrived in a few months' time, they would gift him an abundance of crisp leaves in which he could jump around.

However, there was something that the trees in the Carmichaels' garden did not offer: they would not bear Michael any fruit.

When he was clambering up one of the trees though, he noticed from his new height as he glanced over the fence that the trees in Old Lady Jenkins's garden definitely did provide fruit. Lots and lot of luscious fruit.

Of course, Michael had eaten fruit before. The fruit bowl in their new kitchen was well stocked with apples and bananas and kiwis and peaches. There was never any shortage of fruit in the Carmichael household. He had no reason to sample Old Lady Jenkins's apples.

However, sample one he did.

Michael's mouth salivated as he found himself shimmying across the branch, making his way closer to the fence that separated the neighbouring gardens. There was something about those particular apples, with their shiny, bright red skins, that lured Michael closer. He simply had to try one. He loved apples, and those ones looked especially delicious.

Reaching out his arm, Michael couldn't quite grasp onto any of the fruit. Shuffling forwards a little further, until he was dangerously close to toppling off the branch, he flexed his fingers and leaned over until he could tickle at the fruit. He held on tightly to the branch with one hand and lunged his body forwards until he grabbed hold of the nearest apple. With a slight tug, it came loose from its own branch.

Michael gripped proudly onto his prize as he shuffled back across the branch until he was nestled near the trunk, out of sight of any prying eyes.

However, although Old Lady Jenkins could no longer see the

boy as she looked out across her garden from her kitchen window, she had most certainly been able to see him help himself to one of her precious apples.

Old Lady Jenkins was very proud of both her fruit and her jam, and she worked exceptionally hard to make sure that they grew to perfection, and with a taste to match. It was abhorrent that this slimy worm of a child should steal fruit from her tree.

As Michael greedily bit into the crunchy exterior, sinking his teeth into the sweet yet tangy soft inside of the apple from his hideout, Old Lady Jenkins decided to not take any serious action at this time. A simple word with the mother was surely going to be enough.

'Old La—I mean, Miss Jenkins. What a lovely surprise!' Mrs Carmichael babbled as she opened the front door to reveal Old Lady Jenkins standing there later that evening. Despite having only lived on Nettle Row for a short while, she was already more than familiar with the many stories about her neighbour that circulated the neighbourhood. 'I was going to come over and introduce myself, only I—'

'There is no need for that,' Old Lady Jenkins replied plainly, before getting straight to the point. 'I believe your boy took something from my tree today. He took one of my apples. And then he ate it.'

'Michael did? Oh, I don't think he would do that—'

'Are you calling me a liar?'

'Oh, no. Of course not. I—'

'I must ask that you have a word with the boy and ensure that he does not do it again. I depend on my fruit for my income; I am sure you will have heard by now that that I provide Mr Darwen the shopkeeper with my jam. I cannot afford to have anybody stealing my fruit.'

She emphasised the word *stealing*, causing Mrs Carmichael's eyes to widen.

'Oh, yes, of course, Miss Jenkins. I completely understand. I promise it won't happen again.'

Mrs Carmichael did not hesitate in closing the door as soon as Old Lady Jenkins showed the slightest sign of turning around to head back down the Carmichaels' path.

Of course, Mrs Carmichael, if only because she was more terrified of their neighbour than she had expected herself to be, did warn her son. But Michael had always been an unruly child, and his mother's word rarely meant anything to him. Besides, he wasn't afraid of a silly old lady. Who was she to tell him what he could and could not do? She didn't scare him.

Over the next few weeks, Old Lady Jenkins closely monitored the fruit on her tree as they readied themselves to drop to the ground, ripened to perfection. For a few days, she neither saw nor heard anything of the child. She had seen the family bundle luggage into the back of their four-by-four, and so she assumed that they had went on vacation for the weekend. Her apples were safe. Her jam would not be affected.

Before long though, the Carmichaels returned. Barely half an hour had passed since she had observed their car pulling into the driveway when she heard the young boy squealing his way around his garden. Rushing as much as the exhausted old lady could, she quickly made her way into the kitchen, pulled up a stool by the window, and waited for the dreaded inevitable.

Sure enough, a short while later, Michael clambered back up the tree, shuffled along the branch, and helped himself to another apple. He didn't wait to take a bite this time, munching on the flesh before making his way back down to the ground. Old Lady Jenkins released a soft sigh. This would never do. The child must be taught a lesson, and since the parents did not seem to care that their son was a thief, a dirty criminal who apparently thought he could take as many of her delicious apples as he wanted, then it was down to Old Lady Jenkins to teach him that lesson.

Unfortunately, it would mean the loss of a batch of apples, but it was the price she was going to have to pay. She would just have to provide Mr Darwen with extra jars of plum jam this season instead. The boy's behaviour simply had to be nipped in the bud.

The next morning, Old Lady Jenkins rose early and lit the fire in the kitchen. She boiled an egg for breakfast, and allowed herself the time to enjoy her cup of tea before getting to work. The potion would take all day to brew, and, if she wasn't mistaken, the child would be returning home from school just as it was ready. It was a tight schedule, but there was just enough time.

If she was honest with herself, Old Lady Jenkins was not

entirely confident that this was going to work. It was a potion that she had never used before. In fact, as she prised open the dusty pages of the heavy spell book that had remained untouched under her bed for more years than she could remember, she couldn't recall the last time she had needed to refer to the *Dark Witches' Book of Revenge Recipes*. She would have been a young woman then, she was sure.

However, as long as she worked hard and followed the recipe exactly, then there was no reason why it shouldn't do as it was intended to. She propped the book up on the kitchen table and ran her finger down the list of ingredients. To her relief, she had everything she needed in the pantry, though she would have to make a note to brew more oil of batwing later in the week as she was running out, and the bags under her eyes needed to be kept at bay.

She tied her white apron around her waist and plucked out all of the bottles that she would need from the pantry. The last one to come out was the decanter of whiskrat grout that had been there since before Old Lady Jenkins was born. Maybe even before her mother was born.

With only the sound of the crackling fire embers penetrating the otherwise silent kitchen, Old Lady Jenkins rolled up her sleeves and set about adding splashes of this potion and a dropperful from that bottle, stirring and mixing as the liquid bubbled and boiled at the bottom of the cauldron. It smelt quite warm and sugary, like sweet vanilla buttercream but with a hint of strawberry. It would make a lovely fragrance for her home, Old Lady Jenkins thought. It was almost a shame to add the final ingredient.

Almost, but not quite.

With a steady hand, she reached for the decanter, placing its glass bottom in the palm of her other hand as she carried its weight with caution over to the cauldron. The recipe called for only a tablespoon of the syrup to be added to the thin potion. She removed the glass stopper from the decanter and dripped out a dollop of the gloopy syrup onto a clean spoon. The spoon itself would need to be heavily sanitised after use. Maybe even binned. Or burned.

The boiling liquid sizzled as the whiskrat grout was added into the mixture. Old Lady Jenkins worked her elbows as she used both hands to stir with the spoon until everything blended together into one thick, murky brown potion at the bottom of the cauldron. All she had to do now was let it ferment for a few hours above the flames, and the magic could take effect.

Sure enough, with barely half an hour to go until the boy would be home, Old Lady Jenkins checked on the potion to find that it had blackened to a shade darker than the darkest night, just as the spell book had indicated. With an old ladle, she took care as she spooned the mixture out into a jar and tucked it under her cardigan.

The back door from the kitchen creaked as she pulled it open. The long grass brushed around her ankles as her bare feet padded across the garden towards the apple tree. She paused to lift the jar out of her cardigan pocket before crouching down to the ground.

She used her back to shield her actions from any prying eyes as she tilted the bottle until the potion crept towards the lip. The spell book had informed her to pour the entire mixture onto an absorbent surface near the object, or objects, which she wished to smother in its power. She watched as the heavy liquid glooped out in five big drops onto the soil, infiltrating down to the roots of the tree. Almost instantly, it would work its way up the tree trunk and spread across the branches, reaching the core of the apples within a matter of seconds.

Old Lady Jenkins was surprised by a slight rumbling in the ground immediately surrounding the tree as she stepped back, before returning swiftly back indoors and locking herself away again. Certain that the boy would rush out into the garden upon his return, she pulled up her stool again and took her perch in front of the window, hiding safely behind the net curtains as she began her vigil.

Although Michael did run straight outside once he returned from school, flinging off his schoolbag and throwing his jumper on the ground, he did not head straight for Old Lady Jenkins's apple tree. He had devoured a lemon tart in the car on the way home, and was still feeling a little full. However, it was not long before his nose sniffed out the enticing scent of the delicious fruit that hung from the branches over the fence.

His actions were apelike as he bolted up the tree trunk and across the branch halfway up. With terrifying precision he sprang forward, unaware that he was being lured by the potion that now smothered the apples, and flung his arm over the fence. Without hesitation, he latched onto the largest, juiciest apple.

He didn't pause for breath as he gobbled the apple down in a few swift, unnatural bites. He threw the core down onto the ground and held his hand to his stomach as he felt it grumble. He was hungrier than he thought he was. Without thinking, he reached for another apple. Several seconds later, he had finished that one too. He threw the core to the ground. His stomach grumbled. He ate another apple. And then one more after that.

Four apples later, and Michael was beginning to wonder if his stomach wasn't grumbling after all. Perhaps it was trying to tell him something different.

Perhaps it was trying to tell him he felt sick.

And whenever Michael felt sick, he was always told to sip from a glass of water. And so, clambering back down from the tree, he headed indoors and fetched himself a drink. It seemed to do the trick as his stomach calmed down, allowing him to spring back outside almost immediately after as if nothing had ever happened. He had eaten the apples too quickly, that was all. He didn't need to be concerned.

That night, however, as Michael was lying in bed after his mother had come upstairs to kiss him goodnight and turn out his lights, he felt that peculiar grumbling in his stomach again. He had enjoyed a hearty supper of lamb and potatoes, with a large helping of sticky toffee pudding for dessert. His favourite. There was no way he could still be hungry.

He pulled himself upright and propped the pillow up behind his back. As the grumbling continued, a low throb began to pulse just below his belly button. He remembered that his mother always left a glass of water on his nightstand. He sipped at it now, before taking several large gulps that he forced down his throat. He could feel it chilling through him as each gulp hit his stomach, splashing about as if it was empty.

But it couldn't be empty, could it?

A sharp pang stabbed through Michael's navel. For a moment, as he threw his hands onto his stomach, he thought he needed to rush to the toilet. But then he wasn't quite sure. It was a painful sensation he had never felt before. He doubled over on the carpet, folded over on his hands and knees, convinced he was about to throw up. He retched, but nothing happened. He heaved, clutching his stomach with one hand, almost wishing to vomit. Anything to relieve the pain.

He was just about to call out to his parents when something lodged in his throat. It was nothing tangible, nothing he could reach down and grab onto to pull out, but instead it was like a thought had blocked off any sound escaping through his windpipe and out his mouth.

That was when the wriggling started.

At first it was only an intangible sensation as Michael thought his intestines were moving around inside of him. It would be impossible, of course, but he could think of no other explanation.

The wriggling continued, more uncomfortable than painful. Michael lifted up the front of his pyjama top and gasped with a silent scream.

Whatever it was that was wriggling around inside of him was not deep in his stomach as he had thought, but right against the surface of his skin.

He watched, too stunned to move, as he saw the thin creature wriggle around in concentric circles. It was no longer than two inches, and only half an inch thick, but it dashed and darted with swift precision. Michael tried to catch it, slamming his fist into his stomach, but that only caused the pain to intensify.

The creature, or whatever it was, froze.

And then, without warning, it shot up. It dove through Michael's ribcage, bobbing under and over each bone. It hurtled towards his collarbone, tracing its shape before rushing to his throat.

Michael could feel it properly now as it slithered into his windpipe. The seconds passed in slow motion has he felt this slimy anomaly pulsate up his throat towards his mouth. Tiny whisker-like tentacles tickled at the back of Michael's tongue as the thing crawled across the muscle.

Michael's mouth was wide open as he tried to spit the thing out, but in the time that it took him to breathe in and then out just once, the thing launched itself out of Michael's body, landing on the floor with a plop.

However, the thing did not escape on its own. That sharp stabbing pain that had previously resided only in Michael's stomach instantly whooshed into an impossible agony that engulfed his entire body as he felt his organs force their way through his mouth.

The thing, which Michael could now see as it sat on the carpet looked like a fuzzy caterpillar, but bright blue and glowing in appearance, had hooked its arrowed tail onto the end of Michael's small intestines before it had departed his stomach. They spilled out up through his throat, brushing against Michael's teeth as they poured out in a bloody blob onto his bedroom carpet. Had Michael been able to observe himself as a bystander he would have remarked that it was rather reminiscent of the magician he saw at a birthday partly recently who pulled out a long string of coloured cloths out of his mouth.

There was no time for Michael to take any of it in, however, as straight after the small intestines came the large intestines. After them, his bladder plopped out, closely followed by his liver and kidneys, all adding to the sloppy pile of innards that had rushed out of him. The caterpillar thing flopped about as it continued to pull its tail further away from Michael.

A crack sounded from deep within Michael as his ribs smashed and crumbled as his heart was torn from its ligaments. It raced through his throat, but even in those split seconds Michael could feel and sense everything: the continuous pulsing of his heart as it wormed through his throat; the metallic taste of blood as his heart filled his mouth and smashed out of all his teeth; the way his teeth splayed all over the carpet as his heart whizzed out of his mouth and halfway across his bedroom, bouncing like a ball until it landed with a splat.

Its work complete, the parasitic caterpillar whirled a final dance as it manoeuvred around the pile of innards, inspecting the mess to ensure a job well done. It glanced up at Michael, whose eyes had bulged out of their sockets, and whose cheeks had sunken into his face as his jaw had ripped in half. He was now in a heap on the floor beside the bundle of organs, stinking and oozing and soon rotting away.

With a final satisfied smile on its tiny, furry face, the blue caterpillar thing twirled on the spot like a cat kneading its blanket, then curled up and fell fast asleep. It would never wake again, but it knew this; it was born to serve its mistress, and its destiny had been fulfilled. Michael Carmichael would never steal another apple again.

As Old Lady Jenkins next door saw the jar that once held onto the caterpillic liquid flash a bright blue as if illuminated by a thunderstorm, she knew that the potion had worked. Magic had once again triumphed and the boy had learned his lesson.

The boy had dared to think he could do what he pleased. She was so much more powerful than the snivelling brat would ever be, and she had needed him to know this. To know that he could not defy her. He may have stolen her apples, but Old Lady Jenkins had stolen his life.

Nation Alien

The month of Glabor was peak holiday season for the residents of the planet Bakkorglob. Many preferred to enjoy inbound trips, relaxing on the east-coast shingle or soaking up the moonlight in the darker quarters of the seventh volcano. However, the more adventurous among them often decided to spend a week or two exploring other planets and learning about other cultures. Package holidays for families were quite popular, offering all-inclusive spacecraft travel and destination accommodation. However, some Bakkorglobians were a little more thrill-seeking, and chose to turn on the engines of their private ships and see where the journey took them. Two such Bakkorglobians were Blagrag and Glabgar.

Blagrag and Glabgar had been best friends since they attended smogell school together when they were just four zenots old. Blagrag had grown in rank since their smogell days, now donning on his head a silver rod topped with a red shiny ball to indicate his superior position as captain of his Kabborbolg ship, but this division in stature did not prevent them from enjoying their annual holidays together. They were, after all, both Bakkorglobians, and were not going to let a little thing like superiority hinder their friendship.

On this particular occasion, Blagrag and Glabgar had decided to travel further than either of them had ever gone before. Confident they had everything they needed for their two-week vacation, they clambered aboard the Kabborbolg, ensured all the exits were secure, and headed straight for the cockpit to begin their adventure.

'Glib brig glob obi glook, Blagrag?'

('Will you ever install larger seats in here, Blagrag?')

'Tig gon kugsi glook isgu, Glabgar. Bugki ik gust!'

('The seats aren't the problem, Glabgar. It's your expanding waistline!')

True enough, Glabgar was a lover all anything coated in the sweet delicious waxy taste of kirkelg, and every year as he wedged his short, blubbery green body into one of the two slender chairs in the Kabborbolg cockpit, Blagrag delivered the same lecture about how Glabgar really needed to start watching what he put in his mouth. It never made any difference though. As Glabgar reached for his packed lunch and pulled out favourite soggy kirkelg bun, his answer was the same as always:

'Tuk ig ak katavig! Ik zeig mig kogger kekugik.'

('But I'm on holiday! I'm allowed to indulge.')

With his routine sigh, Blagrag provided no verbal response, and instead fastened his own much taller, slender frame into his captain chair before launching the Kabborbolg into flight.

Aside from a little turbulence around the Zegit quarter midway on their journey, their travel to their destination was a pleasant one. Glabgar had gabbled most of the way there, but had finally fallen asleep and filled the cockpit with rumbling snores two hours before they landed. It allowed Blagrag just enough time to work out their schedule for the next two weeks.

Glabgar awoke only as Blagrag was lowering the Kabborbolg down towards the ground. It hummed gently as it slowed to a halt. Blagrag pulled down the blinds on the cockpit window before hauling himself out of the chair. He stretched, his bones – for Bakkorglobians had bones too, though bright yellow in colour – creaking from remaining in the same position for too long.

'Ag ig ekg?'

('Are we here?')

'Gek, Glabgar. Ig ekg! Ogu ket. Te agmokt ik ko gevok Bakkorglobian kog.'

('Yes, Glabgar. We're here! You'll need this. The atmosphere here is too filthy for our Bakkorglobian lungs.')

Blagrag handed Glabgar his helmet. It was almost comical in its form, a perfect fishbowl-like sphere complete with entry hole, into which Blagrag slid his head. It nestled securely around his neck, a strip of rubber-like substance sealing off any possible entrances through which the air outside the ship could penetrate.

Glabgar, who did not quite have a neck as his head and body merged together, squeezed his shapeless cranium into the helmet until his face was almost pressed against the surface.

'Hog ki bok?'

('How do I look?')

'Kogri. Kog ti, ik zei ekbli gurkki.'

('Beautiful. Come on, it's time to explore our new surroundings.')

Glabgar followed Blagrag as he led him out of the cockpit, down the ship's main corridor, and towards the exit. At the push of a pulsing red button, which emitted a subtle yelp whenever it was pressed, the back door sprung open, with a metal walkway gliding out after it. Glabgar and Blagrag, whose two feet each contained five toes, walked barefoot out into the sunlight.

140

'Ik ag grit!'

(*'It's a bit bright!'*)

'Ik ig kog *British Summer*.'

(*'It is known as* British Summer.*'*)

They continued down the walkway until they rested their feet securely on the solid ground. It wasn't as spongy as the ground back on Bakkorglob, and not as bright either. Where the Bakkorglobians were used to a vibrant bright turquoise surface, this planet Earth on which the two Bakkorglobians had landed appeared to be built of a very plain, beige colour, a shade neither Blagrag nor Glabgar had experienced before. It prickled at the skin on the soles of their feet, causing Glabgar to hop slightly as the walkway behind them zoomed back up inside the Kabborbolg safely out of sight.

'Go zi *Britain*?'

(*'So this is* Britain?*'*)

'*England*, gi zag egok. Ik zeek ikga, kot *prime minister*. Ki zak kag ti?'

(*'*England, *if my map reading has been correct. It is part of a small island, governed by a person called a* prime minister. *Shall we see if we can bump into this creature and say hello?'*)

With a nod of the head and an excitable smile, Glabgar followed Blagrag as they waltzed their way through this strange area known to Britons as a cornfield. The sun was warm as it reflected down on their helmets; it was not so hot that their green skin threatened to peel off to reveal their innards, but since Bakkorglobians were used to life without solar warmth, their existence fuelled instead by the Moon of Kargi, it was enough of a change that they definitely felt like they were on vacation.

'Gri kog torg, Blagrag. Gak gekigs?'

('There's not a lot to see here, Blagrag. What did you say the population was?')

'Grokgi fifty-three million *humans* gri *England*, gik agi one ek thirteen octozents og Bakkorglob. Kri gi, kog kigru gabki.'

('Approximately fifty-three million humans *live in* England, *which is around one for every thirteen octozents on Bakkorglob. That is, if my research is correct')*

'Go kri ok *humans* ot. Kro got?'

('But there doesn't appear to be any of these humans *around. What do they look like?')*

'Ko,' began Blagrag, 'gik ek two ge ke two egk uk ak gek kig ug, uk gik kog ag ik ug geg.'

('Well,' began Blagrag, 'they have two feet and two eyes and a mouth like us, but their nose is at the front of their face, not at the back of the head like ours.')

'Ig gok zu!'

('That sounds bizarre!')

Of course, Blagrag had never actually seen a human before. His description was based entirely from his research on the Galaxy Wide Web – or GWW for short. Had they landed in a large English city, they would have undoubtedly come across a human by now, but their rural landing had left them momentarily without company.

However, a few seconds later, as the two Bakkorglobians turned the corner of what they assumed to be the back of an empty building, Blagrag's dream of finally seeing a human in the flesh was about to come true.

'Og zi!'

(*'Oh wow!'*)

'Ik zu, Glabgar. Zuk krigzi!'

(*'I know, Glabgar. They look incredible!'*)

Blagrag and Glabgar stood a few metres away from the two humans, their eyes wide and glistening in delight. They flinched only slightly when these two humans bolted upright from the hay barrels on which they were sitting. They launched into uttering expletives and shouting curses.

'Ig zuk gizki?'

(*'What's it saying?'*)

'Izku gak, Glabgar. Kez gzu zirk. Zurg, ik Blagrag zu garz Bakkorglob...'

(*'I don't know, Glabgar. Let's introduce ourselves. Hello, my name is Blagrag, and I'm from the planet Bakkorglob...'*)

It was at that moment that human number one reached into his back pocket and brandished a gun in Blagrag's direction. At least, Blagrag assumed it was a gun. It closely resembled the rays they stored on the Kabborbolg for safety, except it was a little longer and thinner. The other human reached for his own weapon as they both mumbled and babbled something incomprehensible.

Blagrag took a step forward, with his hands up in front of him. He was just about to explain that he and Glabgar were visitors to the humans' planet, and that they would very much like to get acquainted with their new fellows, when human number two interrupted his train of thought.

'Stay back!' he yelled, thrusting his gun in front of him.

'What are they?' human number one queried through gritted teeth.

'Looks to me like we got ourselves some aliens,' came the other human's reply. Blagrag, who had studied only elementary English before their vacation, caught only the words 'we' and 'aliens'.

'Gi zu—'

(*'Now look here—'*)

But before Blagrag was able to explain his displeasure at being referred to as an alien – he was a proud Bakkorglobian, no more alien than this confusing human race before him – human number one fired a gunshot into the air. A warning that would not sit lightly with Glabgar.

'Go on! Go back to where you came from!' human number one bellowed. 'We don't want no aliens coming over here and stealing our jobs and our women!' He wiped at his brow with the back of his plaid sleeve.

However, Glabgar, who had remained unusually quiet up until this point, shuffled his bulbous frame forward.

'Go zi kanz ak ki, *human*! Blagrag, zi got kazig!'

(*'Don't you shout at me,* human*! Blagrag, I thought you said they were nice creatures!'*)

'Kogiz zi guz.'

(*'They appear to be defected.'*)

As Blagrag stood with his hands clasped nonchalantly behind his back, not phased by the unexpected threats brandished by these two humans, Glabgar took another waddle forward. The two brave, strong, strapping humans suddenly could not keep up their pretence any longer, their fear of this green globular stranger forcing them to take a few hurried steps backwards, never turning their backs on them.

Human number two stumbled over a rock and landed on the ground, his bottom splashing right into a rich, steaming brown puddle of cowpat.

'Gazig ogzi...kevogz.'

('That smell...is revolting.')

Blagrag may have been quite calm at this point, a little disappointed by the humans, but he chose not to rise to their anger as he struggled to block out the smell of cowpat as it infiltrated into his helmet. It was a different story for Glabgar.

When Glabgar was a small Bakkorglobian of just two zenots, his parents had taken a business trip to the planet Bhortants. They were only supposed to be away for a few days, leaving Glabgar in the safe care of his Aunt Bagritz. However, his parents never returned. They were shot down by a rogue gang of Bhortanties.

Glabgar never saw his parents again, and he had from an early age, once he was old enough to understand the violence behind their deaths, developed a severe intolerance to guns. If these two human things thought they would be able to threaten him with their weapons while he was trying to enjoy his annual vacation, they were gravely mistaken.

Human number two paused, his expression vacant as if trying to internally calculate what had just happened to him. Human number one was for that brief moment distracted by his counterpart's misfortune, and struggled to suppress his snigger.

But nobody was going to make a laughing stock out of human number two.

'That's it!' he said as he shifted his body until he was standing upright again. The smell worsened, causing Blagrag to involuntarily raise a hand to the back of his helmet in an attempt to further block it out. He fought the urge to retch.

An intense anger spread across the face of human number two. The Bakkorglobians never would have expected that human flesh could turn so red so quickly. His eyes appeared to bulge – without the aid of any magnifying helmet – and tiny beads of sweat formed on his brow. With a tight fist gripping onto his gun, he took three slow steps in the direction of Glabgar.

'You're dead, alien!'

He raised his gun, about to shoot, but in a split microsecond Glabgar intercepted his action as he grabbed hold of the barrel of the gun and bent it in two towards the sky. The bullet whizzed up towards the clouds, never to be seen again.

'Y—you broke my gun!' was all human number two could say.

'Come on, let's just get out of here,' human number one suggested. He tried to place a hand on the other human's arm, but he brushed him away.

'No way! This is my home! These aliens have no right to be here. I won't let them get out of here alive!'

'Alive,' 'home,' and 'alien' were the only three words that Blagrag caught. But it was three more than the humans would soon be wishing.

'Ig zir, gogzu? Ik zurti. Ak kir zut, tiz kurgz!'

(*Is that so, gentlemen? I beg to differ. And for goodness' sake, do not call me an alien!'*)

That was the final straw for Blagrag. His rage unleashed, he whirled forwards so quickly that a pile of hay whizzed around the four bodies, clouding their visions as he leapt for human number two. To be called an alien was such a derogatory statement. It was unthinkable, despicable. It was so hostile, so inhospitable. After the Bakkorglobians' failed attempt at greeting their new acquaintances with warmth and respect, Blagrag was no longer interested in treating these humans with the respect they clearly did not deserve.

Five minutes later, humans one and two were tied with leather straps onto metal tables inside the Kabborbolg.

'P—please! We didn't mean—'

'Korzi!'

(*'Silence!'*)

At Blagrag's instructions, Glabgar handed him an assortment of tools and equipment from a large, round orange cupboard. Although these tools had no names to the humans, they could see that they closely resembled earthly scalpels, saws, and what looked like a cheese grater.

'What's he going to do with that?!' human number one whimpered.

Human number two was too scared to reply. He had wet himself, and was now sobbing uncontrollably.

Meanwhile, Blagrag worked in silence as he took each tool

from Glabgar, and arranged them on his workstation. He reached for the needle first and, walking slowly around each of the two tables in turn, plunged it into the humans' right arms, releasing a small, fizzing yellow liquid into their bloodstream. Within three seconds, they were both unconscious.

'Zi gorzi ki, Blagrag?'

(*'What happens now, Blagrag?'*)

'Zi kurzu gatz bogr. Ki zudr obzi, Glabgar, zu itzi ogrik.'

(*'It is now time for me to operate. We tried to play nice, Glabgar, but they did not cooperate.'*)

'Ag zu otik zi!'

(*'And they tried to shoot me!'*)

'Gek, Glabgar, gek zit.'

(*'Yes, Glabgar, yes they did.'*)

As Glabgar observed Blagrag in awe, the latter first polished each object with a luminous blue rag, before operating on the humans. He hummed a miscellaneous tune as he worked, which, now that he was no longer wearing his helmet, filled the Kabborbolg with a pleasant melody.

Ten minutes later, his work was complete.

Waking each human up with a slap to the face, Blagrag untied them and instructed Glabgar to help him wheel them over to the extraction tube at the back of the spaceship. The tube was supposed to be used for removing waste from the ship when they had arrived at an intergalactic rest stop, but it would serve Blagrag well on earth too.

'Orzi og zu, Glabgar?'

('Would you like to do the honours, Glabgar?')

'Og, gek iz!'

('Oh, yes please!')

Without hesitation, Glabgar unstrapped each human and tipped them, each one in a groggy state of confusion, down through the extraction tube. Human number one tumbled silently, and the only sound heard was a definite thud as his heavy body landed on the crops as he fell from the heightened base of the spaceship. Human number two, however, had awoken enough just in time to scream all the way down. He collided with his fellow human as he hit the ground.

Blagrag sealed off the extraction tube again, making a mental note to wash it as soon as they landed back on Bakkorglob. It would take a lot of blubber grease to remove the stench of human urine from the metal casing.

'Kir zu itz ogi, Glabgar? Ig kut brig zu bolg, at ki tez!'

('What do you say we cut this vacation short, Glabgar? I don't know about you, but I'm beat!')

It was the best suggestion Glabgar had ever heard.

'Ki zur bizg, Blagrag! At brig ot zugz *humans*?'

('I couldn't agree more, Blagrag! But aren't you disappointed you didn't get to see more humans?')

'Ag tilz, at zentz gob zib kuk zub. Zuh, ok ik kuz bazi ob kod.'

('A little, but perhaps it was not meant to be. Besides, I'm sure there will be other trips to look forward to.')

'Banz it okz!'

('Right you are!')

It was only when Blagrag and Glabgar were once again strapped into their seats in the cockpit, ready to return to Bakkorglob, that it suddenly occurred to Glabgar that he had no idea what exactly Blagrag had done to the two humans whilst he was operating on them.

'Blagrag? Zi ok zu it ozk *humans?*'

('Blagrag? What exactly did you do to the humans*?')*

Blagrag launched the Kabborbolg, its legs folding inwards as it hovered for a moment. A faint beeping sounded from outside the cockpit as the doors were automatically checked and the ship prepared for take-off. A mild vibration reverberated around the ship as it began its ascent back into the higher atmosphere. Blagrag turned the steering stick, locked it into position, and activated the autopilot before he finally responded to Glabgar.

He replied to him casually:

'Ki zu orki ozt urz. Ki ku zib bulz. Okt zun, zir kit zin obz untizs biz. Zir riz okt tuzb orzi. Zu okt *human* it zoki it taznirt.'

(I simply removed the part of them I believed they would miss the most. Don't worry, they will still be able to function in their day to day lives. They just won't be able to reproduce ever again. And any other human *with whom they come into contact will also be affected by the transition.)*

'Zu zer orbizti?'

('You mean it'll just keep spreading?')

'Oh gez, Glabgar. Zer obizti ez orbizi ugt ez ugti *human's* untizs ogtz za zurb igzo. Rezig iz zu, gorz. Goz tez kurgz at guzg. Noz zut et org. Zo *humans* ez goz, ok gok, ok etni orz enz. Zi erz diz og, abzi ezr it, ak orz zor argzin et tiz mizt pozbinz ot ergoz autoznig eiz. Doz wir, Glabgar. Zi borz lakgzi. Ar kez dezi gilzert, ekz relz it orz.'

('Oh yes, Glabgar. It will keep spreading and spreading until each and every human's reproductive organs reek with the putrid, acidic stench of burning innocence. Revenge is ours, my friend. Nobody treats us like aliens and gets away with it. No one species is greater than the other. Now the humans *will never be great, or good, or anything at all ever again. They shall die out, abandoned and forgotten about, and all because they were too arrogant to open their tiny little minds and consider the possibility that different does not automatically mean evil. Do not worry, Glabgar. We shall have the last laugh as they deplete into a meaningless existence, before disintegrating from history altogether. It will soon be as if the humans never existed at all.')*

Printed in Great Britain
by Amazon